**"My suggestion is that we stop fooling around and get this marriage off the ground."**

Tattie's mouth fell open as she sorted through this. "Fooling...?" she asked incredulously.

He lifted a dark eyebrow at her. "You led me to understand you knew what you were getting into, Tattie. And, for what it's worth, your suggestion of a year's grace was a good one. At least we know we can get along pretty well." His mouth quirked. "We don't appear to have any habits that drive each other up the wall." He looked at her with a question in his eyes.

"Lovers could be a different matter."

"My dear Tattie," he murmured with his hands resting lightly on her shoulders and his gaze summing her up from head to toe, "I feel quite sure that it could only enhance our relationship to become lovers. Trust me."

# Lindsay Armstrong

# THE CONSTANTIN MARRIAGE

Wedlocked!

## HARLEQUIN®

TORONTO • NEW YORK • LONDON
AMSTERDAM • PARIS • SYDNEY • HAMBURG
STOCKHOLM • ATHENS • TOKYO • MILAN • MADRID
PRAGUE • WARSAW • BUDAPEST • AUCKLAND

ISBN 0-373-12384-1

THE CONSTANTIN MARRIAGE

First North American Publication 2004.

Copyright © 2002 by Lindsay Armstrong.

This edition published by arrangement with Harlequin Books S.A.

Visit us at www.eHarlequin.com

**Printed in U.S.A.**

# CHAPTER ONE

ALEX CONSTANTIN rifled a hand through his dark hair and glanced at his watch. It was his first wedding anniversary and the time for the celebrations was approaching fast.

He pushed his chair back and swivelled it so that he could watch the sun set over Darwin and the Timor Sea as he thought about the evening ahead. His wife, uncharacteristically, had been more than happy to allow his parents carte blanche in organising the festivities—she was only now due to fly into Darwin.

His mother, not uncharacteristically, had been delighted to take on the task and the family home, one of them, would be polished to within an inch of its life and glowing with flowers. Mountains of delicious food would be in the last stages of preparation for the buffet supper and the long veranda would be cleared for dancing.

So far so good, he thought drily. What his mother had not dreamt, and what he'd only become aware of when she'd blithely dropped by the invitation list earlier in the day, was that she'd invited his ex-mistress, whose name was known to his wife, to be amongst the hundred or so people celebrating his first wedding anniversary...

A discreet knock on the door interrupted his reflections and his devoted secretary, Paula Gibbs, came in with the last of the dictation he had given her—and the slim, colourful gift box he'd asked her to get out of the safe before she left for the day.

'Thanks, Paula,' Alex said, and motioned her to sit down while he signed the letters. He pushed them back across the desk to her and his hand hovered over the present. 'Would you like to see it?'

'I'd love to!'

Alex opened the box, studied the contents for a moment, then with a shrug pushed it across towards Paula.

She picked up the box and let out a little gasp. 'It's beautiful! I knew it would be pearls, but diamonds as well! And Argyle pinks if I'm not mistaken.'

'You're not,' Alex said wryly, and added in answer to the query in his secretary's eye, 'Giving her Constantin pearls would be a bit like giving coals to Newcastle. At least she'll know I had to buy the diamonds.'

Paula closed the box after a last lingering look at the pearl necklace with its beautiful diamond clasp. Then she said firmly, 'But Mrs Constantin isn't like that, I'm sure.'

He replied, after a moment's thought and with a fleeting smile, 'No, Mrs Constantin is not like that at all, Paula.' But he was suddenly and insanely tempted to add—*Would the real Mrs Constantin please stand up?*

He stood up himself instead, because Paula was an ardent fan of his wife, and, anyway, his problems were his alone. But the question was still on his mind as he drove the short few blocks home to the apartment that faced Bicentennial Park and Lameroo Beach. It had been a cause of some amusement for his wife that the Sultan of Brunei was reputed to own the penthouse in the same building. 'Are you in the same class wealth-wise as the Sultan of Brunei, Alex?' she'd asked with a gleam of sparkling fun in her blue eyes.

He'd denied the charge in all honesty, adding that the

Constantin family fortune, added to the Beaufort fortune which she herself had inherited, would probably be less than small change to the Sultan of Brunei and, indeed, the Paspaley family which had pioneered cultured-pearl farming in the Northern Territory and the Kimberley region of Western Australia.

'But you've also done very nicely out of pearls, thank you, haven't you, Alex?' she'd remarked, and added, 'Plus the cattle stations, cruise boats *et al*?'

He'd agreed, but pointed out that she had also done very well out of her family's fortune.

'True.' She'd glanced at him with a question in those stunning blue eyes.

'I only make the point because you seem to hold my family fortune in a certain sort of low esteem,' he'd said. 'Is it because I'm only a first-generation Australian of Greek descent whereas the Beauforts go back to the pioneering roots of this part of the country?'

'Darling,' his wife had said, 'I never make those kind of judgements. The Beauforts may have been around these parts for a long time but your family is a model of propriety compared to some of my ancestors.'

'So why do you look condescending at times?'

She'd shrugged. 'Sorry. Didn't mean to. But perhaps some of your Greek family's customs don't entirely impress me. I'll leave you to work out which one in particular.' And she'd flitted away before he'd had the chance to remind her that her own mother, who had Russian blood in her, had actively participated in the custom she was referring to...

All this was still on his mind as he took the lift to their apartment, and all the illuminated rooms told him that his wife had arrived back from Perth on schedule. In fact, as her bedroom door was open and Sibelius was pouring out *Finlandia* from her CD player, he was able to observe Tatiana Constantin née Beaufort unseen and at his leisure.

She was dressed and applying her make-up. Her dress was long, strapless, and clung to her figure. It was the same cornflower-blue as her eyes and her dark hair was in a loose, shining bob to her shoulders. At five feet two, she was petite with a delicate figure and smooth, pale skin.

But his wife always had an air of vitality about her, often even suppressed excitement. He'd taken it for a girlish attribute at first—she was only twenty-one now—with not a great deal of substance behind it.

Then again, he'd taken a lot about Tatiana Beaufort on face value when he'd allowed his parents and her mother to manoeuvre them into an arranged marriage. So it had come as something of a surprise when she'd told him unemotionally on their wedding night that she was aware of its orchestration. She was even aware that he had a mistress, she even knew her name. And he'd had to revise his opinions of his wife further when she'd suggested that a year's grace for them both might be a good idea. A year, at least, for her to make up her mind whether to make it a real marriage.

He had agreed and, a year later, was still revising his opinions. Yes, there was something irrepressible about Tatiana Beaufort, there probably always would be, but he'd been wrong about the lack of substance. Just how to quantify it was not so simple, however.

There was no doubt she'd made the best of this first year of their 'marriage in name only' or *marriage by contract*, as she'd called it. She'd relished the role of mistress of his several homes, breathing life and comfort and colour into them. She'd entertained with charm and originality. She'd travelled extensively with him and given the appearance of being a proper wife to the outside world, and she'd been genuinely interested in the process of cultivating pearls.

She had also added stature to the Constantin family by means of her charity work. She was a born social worker and she spent a lot of time working unpaid in a legal aid office. The only thing she hadn't done to date to completely fulfil his parents' expectations was to present them with a grandchild. Which, of course, was what it had all been about in the first place.

His parents were deeply family oriented, and it had been a cross to bear that they'd only been able to have one child. Therefore all their hopes rested on him, and they took an abiding interest in every aspect of his life. Occasionally this was claustrophobic and exasperating, but mostly he bore it with equanimity and did his own thing anyway. But when he'd reached thirty and shown no inclination to marry and provide the dynasty with heirs his mother had decided to take matters into her own hands.

From the first suitable girl she'd paraded in front of him, he'd been quite aware of what was going on. He'd even been slightly amused at her ingenuity. Then he'd grown exasperated by her persistence and gone into evasion mode. But this had hurt her feelings and then two things had happened simultaneously—he'd felt guilty and she'd come up with Tatiana Beaufort, the daughter of an old friend of hers. And there was one aspect of the Beaufort girl that had been impossible to ignore. Her family had been pioneers in the Kimberley district of Western Australia—it was a very old, respected name, and she came with two vast cattle stations.

Not that he gave a damn about the old, respected

name, although he'd known his mother would like nothing better than to add a Beaufort to the Constantin family. But the cattle stations were something else... Between them, should he and Tatiana Beaufort marry, they would own a fair slice of the Kimberley and beef prices were in the process of doubling.

He'd still had no plans to actually do it, though, until it had become obvious that if his mother was a matchmaker of some skill, Tatiana's mother, Natalie, was even better. Cool and subtle, she had presented her daughter beautifully, and it was, Alex had decided, rather like sparring with an accomplished business rival. Perhaps, he reasoned, this was why he'd become determined to find out why Natalie Beaufort, whose daughter could have married anyone, had seemed equally determined it should be him.

And finally she'd put her cards on the table. Tatiana, she felt, had been left extremely vulnerable to fortune-hunters since her father had died. Moreover, before her father had died, she'd led a very sheltered life. He'd been a strict, old-fashioned father, apparently, and the result was that Tatiana, although well-educated and very expensively 'finished', had had a mostly convent education with little contact with the real world.

'She could so easily fall into the hands of an unscrupulous man, Alex,' Natalie had said, and shuddered delicately.

Reviewing her daughter's air of breathless anticipation as he had known it at the time, Alex had agreed—although tacitly. 'What about love, though? I'm sure girls like Tatiana believe in love,' he'd added with some cynicism.

Natalie had waved an elegant hand. 'Is there anyone

less wise than a young girl who believes herself in love for the first time?'

He'd raised his eyebrows and agreed with her again, but this time he'd said, 'Maybe, but how do you propose to make her think she's in love with me? In other words, would she agree to an arranged marriage?'

Natalie had taken her time in answering. She'd looked him over comprehensively, then murmured, 'If you couldn't make a young, impressionable girl fall in love with you, Alex Constantin, who could?'

Alex had met her eyes impassively and she'd laughed softly. 'Sorry, but I'm sure it's true. The other thing is, you have your own cattle stations—who would be better placed to take over the running of Beaufort and Carnarvon than you?'

'Mrs Beaufort,' he'd replied rather grimly, 'this is your daughter's future we're talking about, not a couple of cattle stations.'

Natalie had shrugged. 'Your own mother shares my...belief that a well-arranged marriage has as much chance if not more of success than...what else might befall Tatiana.'

'My own mother,' he'd stated, 'has been parading a series of girls before me in the hope that I'll fall in love with one of them.'

'But all of them eminently suitable, I have no doubt.'

'It is still not the same as cold-bloodedly choosing a husband for your daughter,' he'd retorted.

'Then I'll tell you this, Alex. Tatiana is already a little in love with you.'

This had pulled him up short, although he hadn't allowed Natalie Beaufort to see it. And, as he sometimes did, he'd mentioned the matter to his father. George Constantin had handed the reins of the Constantin empire over to him several years previously but he still liked nothing better than to be consulted. Yet it had come as something of a surprise to Alex to learn that his father was as keen as his mother for him to marry Tatiana Beaufort.

'I didn't even know you were aware of what was going on,' he'd told his father with a lurking smile.

George had shrugged and confessed that he'd left all the details up to his wife, but of all the girls she'd found he had to confess that he thought none could hold a candle to Tatiana. She had looks, she was well-bred, apparently virtuous, and she was young enough to accept a gentle moulding into being a suitable wife. 'And,' he'd added, 'your grandmother actually suggested and campaigned for me to marry your mother—look how well that turned out.'

'It's a different day and age now.'

'Maybe.' George had studied him keenly. 'But would I be wrong in assuming that since Flora Simpson returned to her husband marriage has not been on your agenda?'

Alex hadn't replied and George had gone on. 'Your mother and I aren't getting any younger, Alex. We'd given up hope of having children and thought we were past it when you came along. I think nothing means so much to your mother than to see you happy and with a family. Me too. And, if love has…disappointed you, maybe this is the best way. But the decision has to be yours, of course.'

Alex had glanced at him wryly and thought of telling him that due to his connivance he, Alex, now had a breathless girl a little in love with him, he was being pursued by the queen of all matchmakers and he was actually cherishing unworthy thoughts for a man of integrity—Beaufort and Carnarvon to be precise, to add to the Constantin empire.

But it was only human nature, he had assured himself, to wonder what would happen to Beaufort and Carnarvon if they were left to the mercy of a twenty-year-old girl with a mother who had a reputation of having only one use for money and that was to spend it—perhaps that was why they hadn't been left to her in the first place?

Whatever, he thought, coming back to the present as he watched his wife brush her hair vigorously then pause and conduct a few bars of *Finlandia* using her brush as a baton. He'd had to do nothing but go with the flow from that point on. Tatiana had appeared to welcome his attentions and enjoy his company.

On the lovemaking front he'd learnt that she was rather shy. He had strongly suspected she was a virgin and would like to remain one until she was married. But as their relationship had progressed he'd found that she trembled in his arms and enjoyed his kisses. By the time they'd got engaged he'd been sure that, whatever his feelings were, Tatiana Beaufort was more than a 'little' in love with him.

So what had happened? he wondered, not for the first time. She had consistently refused to explain where she'd gained her knowledge of his mistress, and if she'd known all along it was an arranged marriage, why leave it until then to tell him? Had she ever been even a 'little' in love with him?

*Finlandia*, and Tatiana, still armed with her brush, came to a stirring conclusion, then she whirled round and saw him leaning against the doorpost. And in the moment before she spoke he saw the rush of colour that came to her cheeks and the momentary look of vulnerability that came to her eyes. Because she'd been caught conducting an imaginary orchestra, he pondered, or because of him?

'Alex! How long have you been there?' she asked laughingly, almost immediately recovered.

'Long enough to be impressed by your conducting skills.'

'Oh, that's not fair!' she protested. 'I had no idea you were home.'

He straightened. 'Don't be embarrassed, Tattie. I have the urge to do the same sometimes. How was Perth?'

'Lovely.' She sighed. 'Lovely and cool! I had great fun getting out all my winter clothes and sitting in front of a fire. What have you been up to?'

'The same.' He shrugged. 'By the way, happy anniversary!' And he put the gift box into her hand.

She sobered and looked up into his dark eyes. 'I… Alex, you didn't have to get me a present.'

'No,' he agreed.

'Then…why?'

'I'm quite sure your mother and my parents will be dying to know what I bought you. And I'm quite sure they believe you merit a present for being such a good little wife to me, and you have—for the most part.'

Tattie swallowed visibly. 'You're angry,' she said quietly.

'Not angry,' he denied. 'Puzzled. And wondering what is in store for the second year of our marriage or— if there is to be one?' He looked down at her with a thoughtfully raised eyebrow.

Tattie looked away and turned the box over in her hands. 'The thing is, I…haven't made up my mind…yet.'

He smiled satanically. 'Are you asking for another year, Tattie?'

'No.' She squared her shoulders and looked up at him. 'But I would like to discuss it with you and I don't think now is the right time. For one thing we'll be late.' A smile touched her mouth. 'Think how anxious that would make your mother!'

'Very well,' he said after a long, searching moment, and took the gift box out of her hands. 'In the meantime, allow me to do this.' He drew the necklace out of the box and she gasped much as Paula had done as the river of stunning pearls ran through his fingers and the intricate white and pink Argyle diamond clasp caught the overhead light and reflected it radiantly. 'Turn around.'

'Alex,' she breathed, 'it's *beautiful*, but I don't—'

'Tattie, just do as you're told,' he commanded.

'But I'll feel a fraud, Alex,' she protested.

'You are a fraud, Mrs Constantin,' he reminded her, and grinned wickedly as she opened her mouth to accuse him of the same thing. 'No, don't say it. You shouldn't have agreed to this party in the first place if that's how you feel.'

She subsided, then looked frustrated. 'You may be able to twist your mother around your little finger but I can't. She…she just flatly insisted on a party.'

'My dear, if I could twist my mother around my little finger, not to mention *your* mother, neither of us would be in this mess. Since we are, however, I intend to put a good face on it and so should you. Turn around, Tattie.'

She stared at him with her lips parted and confusion in her eyes for a long moment, then did as she was bid.

'There,' he said, and felt her tremble as his fingers touched the skin of her neck. 'Mmm.' He turned her back. 'Perfect,' he murmured. 'Have I told you about strand synergy, Tattie?'

He traced the lie of the pearls down her skin and across the top of her breasts beneath the blue material of her dress and back up to her neck, and he saw her take an unexpected breath.

Then she began to recite, as if it was a lesson she'd learned, 'The art of choosing the right pearls to put together and drilling and knotting them so the strand drapes like a piece of silk rather than dangling around the wearer's neck.'

'You've done your homework,' he said humorously, and turned her again, this time in the direction of her dressing-table mirror. 'What do you think?'

Tattie took another breath as she studied the pearls in the mirror, but he thought that the whole picture was absorbing her more than the pearls themselves, the two of them close together in the mirror.

She closed her eyes suddenly and said, 'Yes, quite perfect. Thank you *so* much.'

But, as her lashes fluttered up, their gazes caught in the mirror. And he saw the surprise in her eyes as he said softly, 'You're quite perfect too, Mrs Constantin, and your skin is a perfect background for these pearls, it has its own beautiful lustre.'

This time he traced the outline of her oval face and looked down her figure in the lovely dress and thought that she really was exquisite in her own way. Like a delicate figurine, smooth and softly curved but at the same time full of life and laughter.

'Give me ten minutes to shower and change,' he said then, wresting his mind from his wife's physical perfections, and went to turn away but paused. 'Tattie, there's one other unfortunate aspect to tonight's party.'

She was standing quite still, as he'd left her, and she blinked a couple of times as if she was having trouble redirecting her attention. 'There is?' she asked a little blankly.

He grimaced. 'I only saw the guest list today when my mother dropped it into the office. Leonie Falconer is on it.'

He stopped and studied her narrowly but perceived no reaction—at first. Then a dawning look of comprehension came to Tatiana.

'You mean...you mean your mistress?' she stammered.

'My ex-mistress,' he replied harshly. 'How that bit of information escaped my mother I'll never know, but—'

'Perhaps she took it for granted that you had reformed since you married me?'

'Quick thinking, Tattie,' he parried swiftly, 'but you yourself gave me to understand you didn't expect me to live like a monk while you made up your mind about this marriage.'

Tatiana flushed and closed her mouth.

'Even so,' Alex went on, after a tense little moment, 'whatever else I am—' he looked fleetingly amused '—parading my mistresses in front of my wife is not one of my vices. But Leonie has chosen to make herself unavailable today—she's not at her office, she's not home and she's not answering her mobile phone—so I felt...honour bound to warn you that I haven't been able to warn *her* off.'

Tatiana drew herself up to her full five feet two. 'How kind of you, Alex,' she said with all the famed Beaufort hauteur she was capable of but hadn't allowed him to

see until after she'd married him, 'but Ms Falconer is
welcome to do her damnedest!'

He raised a wry eyebrow. 'Bravo, Tattie! See you in
ten minutes.'

## CHAPTER TWO

DARWIN, the northernmost city in Australia and named after Charles Darwin, had only two seasons—the wet and the dry. The wet season coincided with spring and summer on the rest of the continent and the dry with autumn and winter, but, since the temperature rarely fell below thirty degrees Celsius during the day, winter was an inappropriate term.

It was early in the dry season as Tatiana Constantin rode beside her husband to her first wedding-anniversary party, reflecting as she sat in the plush cream leather comfort of his blue Jaguar that things could have been worse. It could have been the height of the wet season when the humidity was legendary, flooding and violent storms were common and cyclones often a threat.

How would she have coped, she wondered irration-ally, with that kind of weather on top of the cyclone-like disturbance of mind she was experiencing at the moment? With the kind of weather that, in the few short steps from an air-conditioned car to air-conditioned premises, left you bathed in sweat with your make-up melted and your hair limp?

She glanced at Alex through her lashes. Unlike her, he had been born and bred in Darwin and the ravages of the wet season never seemed to bother him. But men, she reminded herself, didn't have to worry about looking limp and bedraggled. Indeed, men, she added bitterly to herself, had more powers than were altogether good for them. Such as being able to command a mistress to do this or that.

Mind you, always assuming the mistress hadn't gone to ground, she reminded herself with a touch of black humour!

Tattie had never met Leonie Falconer, design jeweller with her own business who did quite a bit of work for Constantin, although she'd had her pointed out a couple of times. There had to be an element of luck in this, Tattie had reasoned, because, although she didn't think Alex would parade his mistresses in front of her, Darwin was not a big city.

And, although she couldn't think favourably of his mistress, a small part of her applauded the woman's bravado. She had obviously accepted the invitation, then put herself out of Alex's reach at least on this the last day that he might have been able to 'warn her off'. But why accept it in the first place? Tattie was forced to ponder. And why would Alex's mother invite her? Not to mention—how lately had Leonie become an *ex*-mistress?

So many imponderables, she thought wistfully, but the greatest of them all was sitting right beside her, driving his beautiful car with such ease and flair towards his parents' Fannie Bay mansion.

Of course he had always been a huge imponderable, if not to say the biggest challenge of her admittedly young life. And she'd cautioned herself from the moment she'd known what was going on to keep her wits about her. Right up until about half an hour ago she'd thought she'd succeeded in this ambition.

A pearl necklace, the feel of his fingers on her skin and her breasts and the shocking discovery that the mere mention of the word *mistress*, ex or otherwise, had caused all her careful strategies to come tumbling down.

To the extent that she wasn't sure whether she loved Alex Constantin to distraction or hated him exceedingly.

She clenched her fists in her lap and wondered how much she'd given away this evening. Twelve months of such self-control, she marvelled, quite possibly lost in a matter of minutes. She visualised again the picture they'd made in the mirror, he with his dark head bent towards her, she still stunned beneath the impact of his personality, and all that usually leashed masculinity in his tall frame flowing through to her.

Had it been her imagination, she mused a little painfully, or wishful thinking? Because he normally kept that side of him very much leashed in all his dealings with her but she had the feeling tonight had been different. If only, she went on to think, the subject of his mistress had not come up in almost the same breath she would have been more sure...

But really—she glanced at him covertly again—there was only so much of the masculine impact of Alex Constantin he could leash from her. Just to be sitting beside him in his austere dark suit and blue shirt, watching him drive his car, was a bit like a body blow.

Not especially good-looking, he was nevertheless vitally attractive. He was tall, fit and athletic, he could be wickedly amused and amusing, he could be quite kind yet devastatingly scornful when the mood was on him. Above all, he could be the quintessential enigma, so that the reason he'd agreed to an arranged marriage with her when he could have had any woman he chose remained a mystery to her.

*Unless,* his reason had been her reason—two vast cattle stations that went by the name of Beaufort and Carnarvon...

'We're here, Tattie.'

She came back to the present with a little jump, to see that her husband had made his statement with false gravity.

'So I see,' she commented, looking at the house blazing with lights and the stream of cars parked in the street. 'Oh, well, what do they say? ''Onward, Christian soldiers''! ''Fight the good fight''—or, something along those lines.'

He laughed and put his fist beneath the point of her chin. 'You are a character, Tattie,' he said affectionately, and added, 'If it's at all possible, just be yourself and have a good time.'

With your mistress in attendance, your mother, who never fails to drop delicate little hints and tips about how to fall pregnant, and *my* mother there, and *you* treating me like a kid you pat on the head—of course!

She didn't say it, but only by the narrowest of margins. She couldn't prevent the serious irony of her fronded blue gaze as it rested on him fleetingly, however. But before he got the chance to remark on it she opened her door and slipped out of the car.

'That is quite a statement, Tatiana,' Natalie Beaufort said to her daughter when they found themselves alone in the powder room together after the fabulous seafood buffet.

Tattie squinted down at her pearls. 'It is lovely, isn't it?'

'It is, but I was thinking more along the lines of the comment it makes on the success of your marriage.'

Tattie observed her mother and spoke without thinking. 'How do you know it's not conscience money?'

Natalie's sculptured eyebrows shot upwards. 'Is it?'

'I could be the last to know—aren't wives supposed to be?'

'You don't seriously believe Alex is being unfaithful to you so early on?' Natalie asked with a frown.

Tattie thought of pointing out that, although she was behaving herself beautifully, Leonie Falconer was amongst the guests tonight. Leonie, who had been reliably revealed to her as Alex's mistress before he'd married her—and she'd had no reason to believe, until tonight, that things had changed.

But although Natalie was her mother—or perhaps because of it—Tattie knew only too well that her mind moved in mysterious ways sometimes. Such as the number of times Natalie had brought her to Darwin over a year ago, ostensibly to catch up with her old friend Irina Constantin but really to position her daughter firmly in Alex Constantin's sights.

Such as Natalie's decision to move to Darwin herself after Tattie's marriage, like some sort of guardian angel, even though she basically considered the place a far-flung outpost of civilisation. And she decided to hold her peace.

'Just kidding,' she said mischievously, and was relieved to see her mother subside. She couldn't keep herself from thinking that there was irony everywhere she turned these days, though. It was her mother who had advised her before her marriage that there were times when men would be men and it was often wiser to ignore the odd fling they might have...

And she found herself watching her now, curiously, as Natalie expertly touched up her make-up. Whereas Alex's mother was dumpy and not greatly into fashion, but with such a warm personality you couldn't help loving her, Natalie was very slim and very trendy. She was also artistic and played the piano beautifully and adored what she called 'café society'.

Whereas George and Irina Constantin rarely left each other's side, Natalie had frequently sought the solace of their Perth home, away from the lifestyle of Beaufort and Carnarvon and Austin Beaufort, taking Tattie with her.

To be honest, Austin Beaufort had not been an easy man to live with, and Tattie could clearly remember asking her mother passionately once how she coped with him.

Natalie had smiled ruefully and replied that there was an art to coping with men, as she would no doubt discover for herself one day, but walking away from them was something they disliked intensely, and it generally brought them round.

And her mother was undeniably quirky, if not to say downright eccentric at times. She was one of the few people who always used Tattie's full name, but when Tattie had asked her if she'd been named after a Russian ancestor her mother had replied that she hadn't. And she'd gone on to say, 'There's no doubt pregnancy brought out the Russian in me, however.'

'Why? How?'

'Well, it can be very heavy-going at times, with lots of ups and downs and a distinctly 1812 cannon-like flavour to it for the finale. I guess that's why the name Tatiana came to mind.'

Only her mother could say things like that and believe she sounded quite logical.

For all this, though, when she was not fencing with her mother on the subject of Alex and her marriage, she mostly loved her mother's quirkiness. And she knew, even if she disagreed with the means, that Natalie had genuinely thought she was protecting her daughter from the dreaded prospect of fortune-hunters, and had genuinely thought she was in love with Alex.

As for disagreeing with her means, that wasn't entirely true, Tattie forced herself to acknowledge. Because what her mother knew, but few people suspected, was how much of Austin Beaufort there was in his daughter beneath the gloss. And how much of that pioneering Beaufort blood ran in Tattie's veins, so that Beaufort and Carnarvon meant an awful lot to her, and she'd inherited his almost mystical affinity with the Kimberley country they spread over.

Natalie knew how it had affected Tattie to see both properties start to run down during the last few years of her father's ill-health before his death, and had sensed the moment of panic that had come to her daughter to discover, on her father's death, that the responsibility for them now rested squarely on her shoulders. Mystic affinity was one thing. Running two cattle stations that covered the size of the United Kingdom was another.

From that point of view Alex Constantin had been an inspired choice on her mother's part. It had also been, Tattie knew, why she'd gone along with the charade even after she'd realised she was being steered into marriage with a man who wasn't in love with her. It had not had anything to do with the fact that she'd been more than a little in love with him. She would never do anything as essentially wet as marrying a man in the hope that she could make him fall in love with her...

'Penny for them, my sweet?' Natalie patted her fashionable bronze hair and stood up.

Tattie blinked. 'Uh...she's very attractive, Leonie Falconer, isn't she?'

'Certainly very golden. She's a brilliant jewellery designer, I believe, but since she works with Alex you probably know more about her than I do.'

Yes and no, Tattie replied internally. I seem to be the only one tonight who knows she is—or was—his mistress. What I don't know is why I should be alone in the possession of this knowledge. Perhaps I should be applauding how discreet they've been instead of worrying about it?

Her internal monologue was interrupted as her mother gave her hair one last pat and moved towards the door, saying, 'I wouldn't be surprised if she designed the clasp of your pearls—why don't you ask her?'

One of the things Tattie loved about Darwin was its cosmopolitan population. In the space of half an hour she danced with a Danish boat-builder, met a Chinese couple who owned a popular restaurant and a New Zealander who made stainless-steel carvings, as well as a Japanese woman who designed clothes.

Nor could she fault her mother-in-law's party-giving talents. Now the food had been disposed of, the long veranda glowed beneath fairy lights, and the air was fragrant with the heady perfume of what must have been a truckload of roses and orchids in all colours. The guests were colourful and, having wined and dined superbly, were set to dance the night away. It was an extremely successful party.

At all times, however, it was as if Tattie possessed an unseen pair of antennae tuned in exclusively to Alex and Leonie. So far her antennae had picked up no communication between them at all. Then she looked around and found Leonie standing directly behind her, apparently admiring the clasp of her pearls.

'Oh. Hello,' Tattie said brightly. 'We've never met

but I know who you are—do I have you to thank for
my clasp?'

Leonie Falconer possessed hazel eyes, long gold hair
and a statuesque figure presently clad in a beautiful
gown of gauzy fabric shot with all the colours of the
rainbow. She too wore pearls—Constantin? Tattie wondered—and a chunky, very lovely gold bracelet.

But all this was on the periphery of Tattie's mind as
she watched those hazel eyes narrow with a slight wariness then relax as she finished speaking.

'No,' Leonie said in a husky, transatlantic voice. 'Not
my work, but rather nice all the same.'

'Thank you!' Tattie looked around and, observing
Alex nowhere in sight, added quietly, 'Why did you
come tonight, Miss Falconer?'

Leonie Falconer resumed her wariness rather abruptly.
She was in her late twenties, early thirties, Tattie judged.
She was also several inches taller than Tattie, but none
of that prevented Tattie from eyeing her severely and
imperiously.

A tinge of colour ran beneath Leonie's honey-gold
skin, then she shrugged. 'Curiosity, I suppose. Why
would I be invited in the first place? Also—'

'I can tell you that,' Tattie interposed swiftly, 'Irina
organised this party. Alex was unaware until today that
you had been invited. So was I. And Irina was definitely
unaware of who you were, otherwise she wouldn't have
touched you with a bargepole.'

'I see.' Leonie looked fleetingly amused then oddly
bitter. 'Well, there's no reason I shouldn't be here, as it
happens. I got my marching orders some time ago. And
marching orders they were too—*Any fuss, Leonie, and
Constantin will cease to do business with you.* I'm sure
I don't have to tell you how deadly Alex can be when

he sets his mind to it. But when his brief infatuation with you ceases, *Mrs Constantin*,' Leonie added silkily, 'I'll get him back.' And she turned on her heel and walked away.

'What was all that about?'

Tattie jumped and found her husband standing beside her. 'Probably an age-old ritual between mistress and wife, Alex,' she said coolly, then her lips trembled and she laughed softly. 'But how bizarre that you should use me to extricate yourself from her.'

'What do you mean?' he said rather grimly.

Tattie opened her mouth then caught sight out of the corner of her eye of his mother, radiant in pink silk that didn't suit her at all but didn't manage to dim her personality either, approaching them with a slight limp. She sighed inwardly and said, 'Don't worry about it, Alex, but I think you should dance with me in a very husbandly way now, if for no other reason than to let your mother think her party is a real success!' And she melted into his arms.

Surprise kept him rigid for a moment. And he said barely audibly, 'You're going to have to explain later, you know, Tatiana.' Then he drew her into his arms and, despite the implicit threat in the use of her proper name that always told her he was in a dangerous mood, kissed her lightly before swinging her round to the music.

'I think I'll go to bed now, Alex,' Tattie said at two-thirty in the morning, after a swift silent ride home at the end of the party.

She had preceded him into the lounge, a lovely room she had created in their apartment—the apartment he had bought and presented to her as a wedding present in accordance with the contracts he and her mother had agreed upon—with a view through the wide windows to the terrace. The view was dark now, of course, but the oil rig anchored in Darwin Harbour for maintenance was lit up like a Christmas tree.

'Oh, no, you don't, Tattie.'

She stopped in the middle of the lounge and turned to look at him. She had her shoes in one hand, her pearls in the other and her face was shadowed with weariness. 'Alex, this is no time—'

'Sit down, Tattie,' he ordered, and came across to her with two tall glasses in his hands.

'What's this?' she queried as he handed her one.

'Something long, cool and delicious for someone who has partied as vigorously as you have. Don't worry, I'm not planning to make you drunk and seduce you.' He looked down at her wide eyes and slightly apprehensive expression.

Tattie took the glass from him, drank deeply as if she was very thirsty, then in a stiff little voice recounted her conversation with his mistress. And she sat down abruptly.

Alex lounged against a pillar and merely twisted his glass in his hands. 'What she told you is not an accurate representation of the events.'

Tattie went to wave her hand and realised she was still clutching her pearls. She put them down carefully. 'It doesn't matter one way or the other to me, Alex.'

'I would have thought it might in the light of how we go on, Tattie. You did say you wanted to discuss that with me.'

'Well. Yes. But...' She trailed off, looking almost ashen with weariness and strain now. 'I can't think straight.'

He took his time. He sipped his drink then he said

quietly, 'My suggestion is that we stop fooling around and get this marriage off the ground.'

Tattie's mouth fell open as she sorted through this. 'Fooling...?' she said incredulously, picking on perhaps the least startling aspect of his advice.

'Or whatever you like to call it.' He looked briefly quizzical.

'You know what I like to call it, Alex.'

He lifted an eyebrow at her. 'You also gave me to understand that you knew what you were getting into, Tattie. But, for what it's worth, your suggestion of a year's grace was a good one. At least we know now that we can get along pretty well.' His mouth quirked. 'We don't appear to have any habits that drive each other up the wall.' He looked at her with a question in his eyes.

'That's...assuming we were brother and sister, Alex. Lovers could be a different matter.'

He put his glass down on a beautiful, inlaid pedestal table and came over to her. She stared up at him wide-eyed as he removed her glass from her fingers then drew her to her feet.

'My dear Tattie,' he murmured with his hands resting lightly on her shoulders and his gaze summing her up from head to toe, 'I feel quite sure that it could only enhance our relationship to become lovers. Trust me.'

His fingers slipped from her shoulder to trace the line where his pearls would have lain and, despite her tiredness and confusion, she couldn't help the reaction that came to her again, that trembling sensation any close contact with him brought to the surface.

'But sleep on it,' he suggested.

'I...' She bit her lip.

'I'm off on a tour of the pearl farms early tomorrow,' he continued. 'I'll be away for a few days. So you'll be able to do more than sleep on it.' He kissed her lightly on the top of her head. 'I thought, after that, we could spend a little while at Beaufort. I have some ideas for it.'

Sheer blackmail!

Tattie sat up, saw it was nine o'clock in the morning and clutched her head as the blackmail thought raced through her mind.

Tired as she'd been, sleep had been difficult, and when she'd achieved it weird dreams populated by Leonie Falconer resembling some sort of smug sun goddess had plagued her. So why had she woken up with blackmail on her mind?

Because apart from her mother only Alex knew how close to her heart Beaufort especially was. How could he not? True, she'd been fascinated by the cultured-pearl side of his business—she would have loved to be visiting the farms with him—but it was his cattle stations and how he handled them that she had attempted to absorb like blotting paper. All for the purpose of applying that knowledge to Beaufort and Carnarvon should she ever have to run them on her own.

But, more than that, perhaps only Alex guessed that twelve months had not been long enough for her to have the confidence to run them on her own and that was why he'd applied the sheer blackmail of promising her some of his time at Beaufort and mentioning the ideas he had for the station. What else could she think?

'You could ask yourself why he wants to stay married to you, Tatiana,' she murmured, and lay back with a sigh.

Had the impossible, the wonderful, the dream within a dream that she hadn't dared to allow herself to dream,

come true? Had her husband finally fallen in love with
her? Or had the time come to amalgamate her inheri-
tance with his into one big cattle operation, something
that had not happened to date?

Why, she pondered gloomily, did that seem much
more likely?

And she answered herself tartly, he made her feel like
a kid, not—apart from one fleeting moment yesterday
and she wasn't even sure about that—a woman he found
desirable. It was as simple as that.

On the other hand—she sat up again, struck by a new
thought—why had he divested himself of his mistress?
Because of a growing but *hidden* attraction to her—or
so she would have no ammunition with which to continue the stalemate or base a decision to leave him on?

Her bedside phone rang. She stared at it, then lifted it
reluctantly.

'Hello?'

'Tattie?' her mother-in-law said down the line in a
slightly overwrought way. 'My dear, that was the best
party I've ever given and all thanks to you!'

Tattie frowned. 'No way, Irina. I didn't do anything;
you did it all.'

'But you were there, you were so lovely, and the
whole world could see that you and Alex are perfect for
each other—I just wanted to tell you! Perhaps next year,'
she added, 'we will have a little addition to the family
to celebrate? Tattie…' There was a slightly awkward
pause down the line—an indication of a bull being taken
by the horns as it turned out. 'Are there any problems
in that direction? Because I have the best gynaecologist
in the country, the most understanding, most gentle,
most kind, and he has performed miracles for several of
my friends' daughters.'

This time Tattie grimaced, then drew a deep breath. 'Irina…' But she couldn't do it. She simply couldn't dent her mother-in-law's enthusiasm and her old-fashioned belief that her arranged marriage concept had worked blissfully—although it did cross her mind to say, Perhaps you should have found a Greek girl for Alex. A girl who would understand these things and know where her duty lies…

She cleared her throat. 'Uh—Irina, no, no problems that I know of, but this is between Alex and me, I feel…I *really* feel, don't you?'

There was silence, then, 'My dear, forgive me,' Irina said a little tremulously down the line. 'Of course it is. It's just that I have such a longing for grandchildren and, sadly, I'm not getting any younger.'

'Irina…' What to say? Tattie thought desperately, because in every other respect Irina had been a lovely mother-in-law. Nor *was* she getting any younger, and she was also plagued by a troublesome hip, but kept putting off a hip replacement because of her fear of hospitals and operations.

She was saved by Irina herself, who said bravely, with less tremolo, 'I promise not to mention these things again, Tattie. I just… Last night…seeing you and Alex…I got carried away. Forgive me?'

'Of course,' Tattie said warmly. 'Tell you what, why don't we have lunch? I'll ring Mum and see if she can make it as well and we can have a gorgeous gossip about the party. How about Cullen Bay?' She named a restaurant.

She put the phone down eventually, wondering as she did if she wasn't digging a deeper grave to have to climb out of one day. Then she lay back and switched on her television, only to be arrested as she flicked through the channels by a programme about an Indian family in Mauritius. What arrested her was the fact that the patriarch still chose husbands and wives for his family, even sending to India for them, and the whole family laughingly agreed it was still the best way to go.

She tightened her mouth, switched off and got up to take a shower. While the shower refreshed her body the circles of her mind ran around a familiar pattern. Why *hadn't* the Constantins sought a Greek girl for Alex? She knew enough about the continental community in Darwin to know that it wasn't only amongst Mauritian Indians that this practice was common. She could even see a certain sense to it. Same culture, same background—possibly the same expectations.

But Alex was about as cosmopolitan as they came— or, to put it another way, he was as Australian as they came. So perhaps he wouldn't have stood for it?

A smile crossed her lips at this point in her reflections but it was gone almost before it was born—Alex did exactly as he pleased, she knew, despite his affection for his parents. So had they been, as she'd long suspected, rather clever? Had they found the one lure he'd been unable to resist in their quest to further the dynasty?

A little dialogue ran though her head, *no matter that the girl is not one of us. She still looks to be pliable, and she does have Beaufort and Carnarvon—could he resist that?* Could he?

'Perhaps not,' she answered herself, and started to dress.

It was yet another bright, cloudless July day, but it passed by in a bit of a blur for Tattie.

Her cleaning lady arrived as she was having her breakfast coffee, and together they went through the

apartment, deciding what needed to be done. Then Tattie
went back to her coffee, but the apartment stayed on her
mind and she looked around with new eyes.

She'd chosen pastels, light, airy colours that were
above all cool. There were no curtains but wooden lou-
vers at the windows, and she'd made simple but effective
statements—a glorious oil painting on a feature wall; a
pair of waist-high porcelain urns hand-painted in soft
pinks, gold and royal blue; an intricately carved solid
silver bowl it was hard to take your eyes from, so perfect
were its proportions and soft old glow as it sat on a small
sea chest; a vast, comfortable cream couch lined with
pink and pewter cushions.

Mysteriously, she thought with a sudden pang, it had
all become home. Yes, of course the lure of the
Kimberley region where her ancestral home was, a
sprawling, rambling country homestead, still held pride
of place in her heart—or did it? And if not, why not?

Because this was her own creation? she wondered.
Because this was where she and Alex spent most of their
time? There was also a house in Perth, another house in
Darwin and an apartment in Sydney, but, even though
she'd added her own touches to those, this apartment in
Darwin was all hers—and Alex's.

She took up her cup and wandered into his bedroom.
Not that he'd known until their wedding night that this
room was to be his and the main bedroom would be
reserved for her exclusive use. And what kind of a gamble had that been? she paused to ask herself as she remembered how her wedding day had passed in a fever
of nerves. Nerves and the terror that she might have
made an awful mistake, only to discover that the equanimity with which he'd heard her out and accepted her

proposal had killed a silly little ray of hope in her heart...

Nor would she forget the humorous quirk to his mouth and the glint of devilry in his eyes as he'd surveyed this bedroom on that night. Because, luxurious though it was, it contained a single bed—a king-size single not much smaller than a double, but nevertheless, perhaps a ridiculous gesture on her part, she brooded. Not to mention a sheer nuisance, since she'd had to get all its bedding custom-made, king-single linen to match her dusky-blue and pearl decor being impossible to come by.

She grimaced. Young and stupid she'd been, but was she only now about to discover just how young and stupid? She'd certainly had an inkling, as the milestone of her first anniversary approached and she'd found herself unable to come to any decision about her marriage, that—what? She was staring down the barrel of a gun? That she'd foolishly expected *something* to crop up, some resolution to present itself, only to find that she was still at square one?

If only she could find the key to the enigma that was Alex Constantin, she thought a little wildly, and walked into the room. The bed was unmade, but otherwise it was fairly tidy. He'd hung up his suit from the night before, his shirt was in the linen basket; only his tie was carelessly discarded over the back of a blue velvet chair. She picked it up and sat down on the bed, running the length of silk through her fingers.

Other than an exquisite pearl shell on the bureau, Alex had brought nothing to this room. No photos or memorabilia from his pre-marriage days. And his study in the apartment was the same. Functional, sometimes untidy, but essentially impersonal—so much so it was she who had added some blown-up photos of the beautiful bays and rivers that housed his pearl farms. Was he just that kind of man or were his treasures and mementoes stored elsewhere? At the Fannie Bay house of his parents? At— she shivered suddenly—a separate residence he maintained for entertaining his mistress?

I won't do it, she thought abruptly, and got up to hang his tie on the tie rack in his cupboard. I won't agree to a real marriage with Alex Constantin until I know without doubt that he is...*madly* in love with me!

She stared at his ties rebelliously, then went to change for her lunch date with his mother.

# CHAPTER THREE

FOUR days later Tattie was no further forward in her decision-making process and not sure when to expect Alex back. He'd gone on to Broome, apparently. But she'd kept herself busy, spending most of her days in the legal-aid office where she played the role of receptionist but spent a lot of time listening to other people's problems and trying to give sound advice.

It was a Wednesday morning before she left for work when she discovered an invitation in her mailbox from a friend who was having an impromptu luncheon at a popular café in Parap that day. It had been hand-delivered. It crossed her mind to wonder why Amy Goodall, whom she'd been to school with in Perth and was now living in Darwin, hadn't simply rung her, but she shrugged as she tossed the colourful little invitation on the hall table. Amy had always been unconventional and given to springing surprises on people, and an hour of her stimulating company and others' would be fun.

So she dressed with a little more care than normal for work in a stunningly simple sleeveless white piqué dress, black and white sandals and a loop of black and white beads. She brushed her hair vigorously and drew it back into a white scrunchie, and with a lighter step descended to the garage and her racy little silver Volkswagen Golf convertible.

At twelve-thirty she drove to the Parap shopping centre with its leafy boulevards, parked the Golf under a magnificent poinciana tree and stepped out to be confronted by a man who appeared from nowhere.

'Mrs Constantin?'

'Yes,' Tattie said uncertainly, and with a strange feeling at the pit of her stomach. He was tall, he looked as if he hadn't shaved for days, and he had angry blue eyes and matted curly hair. He was also completely unknown to her.

'Just do as I say, Mrs Constantin,' he recommended, and pulled a small gun from the pocket of his jacket.

Her eyes dilated and her heart leapt into her throat. 'What on *earth*—' she began.

'Come with me nice and quiet so I don't have to use this, which I will if I have to.'

'I...I...' But as she stammered and felt like fainting he took her elbow in a hard grasp and began to lead her towards a battered utility parked two spots away from the Golf.

She stumbled and tried to pull her elbow free but he growled an obscenity into her ear. She sucked some air into her lungs and opened her mouth to scream, but she felt the gun poke into her waist—and nothing came out of her mouth. Then all hell broke loose.

A car screeched to a halt in the middle of the road only a few feet from them—a blue Jaguar—and Alex jumped out without bothering to switch off the engine.

Her attacker immediately pulled her in front of him and swore viciously but Tattie buckled at the knees, wrenched her elbow free and threw herself sideways. Alex leapt on the man and punched him to the ground in a hail of devastating blows.

Tattie got to her knees as they rolled away from her, saw the gun on the ground and fell on it, but her assailant was no match for Alex—he was being mercilessly subdued in a show of brute strength that made Tattie blink. Then there were sirens and police swarming around them. Finally Alex, still breathing heavily, was helping her to her feet.

'What...? I don't understand... Oh, you're bleeding!'

'It's nothing, Tattie. Are *you* OK?'

'Yes, I think so, but...why...what?' she gasped.

He held her close for a moment then said gently, 'Come, I'll explain when we get home.'

Three policeman had accompanied them and now listened intently to Alex's explanation.

'When I got home today I noticed this invitation on the hall table.' He lifted Amy's colourful little card. 'But it so happens I ran into Amy Goodall at the airport this morning and we had a bit of a chat. I was on my way home from Broome, she was on her way to Sydney, so it made no sense that she would be inviting my wife to lunch today. I also noticed that the invitation had been hand-delivered.' He proffered the envelope. 'And it occurred to me that someone might have deliberately lured my wife out on a false pretext.'

Tattie made a strange little sound of disbelief.

'And that's when you rang us,' the detective in charge murmured. 'Only you got there before us. Mrs Constantin, did you recognise the man at all?'

'No! I've never seen him before.'

'Did you find this invitation at all strange?'

Tattie shrugged. 'I wondered why she hadn't rung, that's all. But she is that kind of person, prone to springing surprises.'

'So it would be fair to say the gentleman we've taken into custody must be aware of Miss Goodall's quirks.

How well do you know her, incidentally, Mrs Constantin?'

Tattie told him.

'And you don't think she could have had anything to do with this?'

'Good heavens, no! Anyway, she's on her way down south.'

'Yes,' the detective said thoughtfully, and looked at Alex. 'The obvious thing that springs to mind is kidnapping for ransom.'

Tattie gasped, and if she hadn't already been sitting down would have collapsed.

Alex said then, 'I think my wife has had enough for the moment.'

As soon as the police had left, Tattie said one of the sillier things she'd ever said as she looked at Alex wide-eyed and still stunned.

'Why would anyone want to kidnap me?'

He came to sit down beside her. There was a darkening bruise on his cheek, his shirt was torn, his knuckles grazed, but the cut on his arm had stopped bleeding. For that matter, her lovely white dress was stained, her knees were grazed, her scrunchie was hanging by a thread of hair and her face was dirty.

He half smiled and gently removed the scrunchie. 'Why? I have rather a lot of money, Tattie.'

She swallowed. 'Thank heavens you came home and saw the invitation. Thank heavens you bumped into Amy! I didn't know what to do. Part of me was thinking, surely he wouldn't shoot me in broad daylight in the middle of Parap, but the other half couldn't be sure. It... I...'

'Tattie.' He took her in his arms. 'I can imagine. And

if it's any consolation I doubt whether he would have shot you in the middle of Parap, but he's safely under lock and key now.'

'Maybe there are more of them!' She shivered in his arms.

'I doubt that too.' He stroked her hair. 'I suspect he was a loner and it wasn't a very well-thought-out plot.'

'Maybe,' she conceded, but couldn't stop shivering.

'Hey,' he said quietly, 'it's over. I'm here.' And he kissed her.

As an antidote to extreme nervous tension, it worked well. The shivering started to subside as his mouth closed on hers, and the incredible events that had befallen her gave way to something else.

How good it felt to be in his arms, how safe—and how ruthless he'd been in her defence, as if she meant an awful lot to him. Then even those thoughts receded and sensations began to take their place. She no longer noticed that she was in a mess. She began to be aware of herself on a different plane altogether, very much as a woman with all the needs and desires of one, most of which he was attending to with his hands and his lips.

He stroked her arms with his long fingers and she shivered quite differently, with delight. He kissed her lightly, then those cool, firm lips sought the soft hollows at the base of her throat while his wandering fingers combed through her hair. But not only was it what he was doing to her, it was the feel of his strong, hard body against hers that filled her with a lovely, special feeling of excitement.

Then he started to kiss her more deeply and she responded, shyly at first, then more and more freely. They drew apart once and she stared at him, suddenly overwhelmingly aware of the sexy side of Alex Constantin as she'd never been before. The mouth-watering masculinity of his wide shoulders and lean hips, the planes of his face, and what being under the gaze of his faintly amused eyes did to her.

It was one thing to be sitting beside him in a car and feel his presence like a body blow, she realised. It was one thing to have been kissed by him during their engagement—most chastely, she now realised. It was entirely another thing to have him focused squarely on her and kissing her with all that latent sexiness very much unleashed. Oh, yes, she thought a little wildly, this was another matter altogether.

'This' brought out the strangest thoughts in her. How glad, for example, she was to be wearing a minuscule but very fetching pair of white lace bikini briefs and a matching bra. How her skin would feel against the cream textured velvet of the couch when he undressed her; how hot, erotic and sexy she felt herself, so that the couch, the carpet, anywhere would be OK for him to make love to her, because she might die a little if he didn't...

Then he slid his hand beneath the hem of her dress and stroked her thigh, and she made absolutely no protests of any kind—and the phone rang.

She thought he swore under his breath. She thought she made a husky little sound of sheer frustration, but in the next moment he'd released her and she was sitting very properly, with her hem tucked around her legs, while he went to answer the phone and the door.

'The police,' he said, coming back to her with his lips twisting to see she hadn't moved a muscle. 'I need to go down to the station but you don't have to come. And you don't have to worry about being alone. The apartment has been put under surveillance just to be on the safe side.'

Tattie licked her lips but found herself with nothing to say.

'Why don't you have a long shower and a rest?' he suggested. 'Or would you like me to call your mother or my mother?'

'No! Uh…no, thank you.' She tried to smile. 'I'd rather not be fussed over at the moment.'

'Tattie.' He sat down beside her and put his arms loosely around her. 'You look as if you've been in an earthquake, and I don't mean physically, although there's that too. But the fact that we both enjoyed that very much has got to help in our marriage, wouldn't you agree?'

Her lips parted but again no sound came.

'Anyway—' he smiled faintly '—think about it. I'll be as quick as I can. And I am going to call your mother and my parents—we can't leave them to hear about it on the radio and I don't think you should be alone.'

He waited until George, Irina and Natalie arrived. It didn't take long for them to rush over. He suffered their concern—his mother thought he might need stitches in his arm—and admiration with a wry little smile.

And for a time after he'd gone Tattie was glad not to be alone. So she let them ply her with tea and cake and generally fuss over her, especially her mother, who kept folding Tattie in her arms. And she went through it all again with them, unaware of how her eyes shone as she described how magnificent Alex had been in her defence.

But all of a sudden she knew she had to be alone, and she told them she was going to have a sleep. It took some determination to persuade them—again, especially her mother—that she would be fine, but finally they left.

*     *     *

She took a bubble bath in the huge, raised marble bath that was fashioned in the shape of a shell in her *en suite* bathroom. The marble was champagne-coloured and all the towels, the soap and bottles were a soft jade-green. It was normally a most relaxing place but, even smothered in bubbles to her chin and with two fragrant candles burning as she soaked away the unusual events of the day, she felt far from relaxed.

Really, she thought, it was too much to be almost kidnapped then subjected to her husband at his dangerously sexy best—a first for her—all in the space of a few hours!

Was it any wonder she couldn't think straight?

And was this why Leonie Falconer was determined to get Alex back? Because his dangerously sexy best was irresistible?

She looked at the pads of her fingers and discovered they were wrinkled. So she got out of the bath before she resembled a prune all over, but her thoughts continued like a string of pearls with synergy—one set of thoughts leading smoothly to the next. No, not smoothly, she contradicted herself, not synergy at all, really, but jumping about like fleas, with all sorts of possibilities for this turn of events presenting themselves...

How long had Alex deliberately deprived himself of his mistress, and did that have anything to do with him needing not necessarily her but any woman?

She would have to put it to him, she felt, although she quailed inwardly at the prospect. Because it was all very well to take these developments at face value, but what protection did that offer her against spending the rest of her life in love with him while he had a series of mistresses once he'd secured her, heirs for the dynasty and, of course, two cattle stations?

She dressed in a long fuchsia skirt, to hide her grazed knees, and a pale rose silky knit top. And, because she didn't have anything else to do, she started to prepare dinner. It was a beautiful evening with the sun setting over Mandorah, so she set the glass table on the veranda—a yellow candle in a glass, frosted yellow wine glasses, and white Rosenthal china with ice-blue place mats and napkins. And her stir-fry beef with oriental rice and a salad was just about ready as Alex came home.

He looked her over, and the meal, forked some of the stir-fry from the pan, told her it was delicious and that if she could give him five minutes for a shower he'd really appreciate it.

'Of course! Take as long as you like; I can keep this warm—'

'Five minutes, Tattie,' he murmured, and kissed her lightly on his way past.

She leant back against the counter and swallowed, because it was all happening to her again: the accelerated pulse, the ragged breathing, patches of dew on her forehead and the deep inner trembling even though his lean body had barely brushed hers. In fact she had to go outside and sit at the table to compose herself.

He brought the meal out and opened a bottle of wine. He'd changed into fresh jeans and a white shirt.

'So?' she said, having fought a stern fight with herself and told herself not to be such a wimp. 'Have they found out who he is and why he did it?'

Alex poured some golden-green liquid into the frosted glasses, then propped the bottle in a wine cooler. 'Yep. He went to water. He was an employee of mine, although we'd never met—a diver. He got sacked for drinking. Then he met Amy Goodall at a party, she let slip that she knew you, so he—cultivated her, you might say. They had a brief affair, but long enough for him to discover how wacky she could be and how that could be used to further his obsession with revenge against me for his sacking.'

' 'And Amy has confirmed all this?' Tattie asked, wide-eyed.

'Amy has told the Sydney police that she did have an affair with him, but she had no idea how he was using her.'

Tattie sat back. 'Does this mean,' she asked with a frown, and sipped her wine, 'I'll have to be on guard against this for the rest of my life?'

Alex lifted the covers from the stir-fry and the rice and inhaled the fragrant steam. 'If you stay married to me, Tattie, we will need to take precautions, but that could be the least of our problems. Will I dish up?'

She nodded dazedly after a moment. 'What do you mean?'

He wielded the stainless-steel serving spoons and handed her a plate. 'If you stay married to me I'll be able to put all the necessary precautions in place. If you don't, you'll still be Tatiana Constantin.'

'Only on my own...oh!'

'Mmm,' he agreed. 'But that is certainly not the only reason for you to overcome your reservations about this marriage.' He sat down. 'And don't tell me there aren't some.'

'How...how did you know?'

A corner of his mouth quirked and the look he sent her was full of irony. 'Tattie, in some respects I have to admit you're a closed book. But when you're concerned or undecided about something I can tell.' He paused and contemplated his meal, then raised his dark eyes to her

with a glint of sheer devilry. 'Although that wasn't altogether the case just before the phone rang.'

A slow tide of colour burnt its way up Tattie's throat
and stained her cheeks, but she wasn't a Beaufort for
nothing. 'How long is it since you've had a woman,
Alex?'

'Ah. A Beaufort counter-attack, I take it?' He laughed
softly. 'I never did meet your father but I've heard he
was a hard man. I wonder if he realised you inherited
some of his famed…quickness on the draw?'

'Perhaps he did,' she said evenly. 'Perhaps that's why
he left me Beaufort and Carnarvon. But I have to tell
you, Alex, that, while I may have got a little…carried
away before the phone rang, it doesn't stop me from
pondering your motives. Out with your mistress; in with
your wife—why?'

'I'll tell you, Tattie,' he said pleasantly. 'Leonie became obsessed with replacing you as my wife, despite
the provenance of our relationship, which was to begin
with, and before I ever met you, that she had no desire
to marry anyone.'

Tattie absorbed this. 'And…and you didn't threaten
her with taking all the Constantin business away from
her?'

'Yes, I did. In fact, I have now done so.'

'W-why?' Tattie stammered.

He looked at her meditatively. 'She shouldn't have
come to our anniversary party.'

'Isn't that a little…hard and unfair?' Tattie postulated.

'Are you taking her side?' he countered. 'Could there
have been any reason for her to come other than to make
mischief?'

'Of course I'm not taking her side, but she might not
have known I knew about her!'

That silenced him for a moment, then, 'How *did* you come to know about her, Tattie?'

Tattie ate the last of her rice and pushed her plate away. 'I have a friend who worked for her. She... thought she was doing me a good turn.'

'I see. And did your friend tell you the whole story?'

Tattie lifted her blue gaze to his. 'I thought so—are you going to tell me she wasn't your mistress?'

'No.' He shrugged. 'But she was not my mistress at the time of our marriage.'

Tattie's mouth fell open.

'Quite so,' he said with a tinge of mockery.

'So what...what...? How...?'

'I'll tell you in the hope that we can put Leonie behind us once and for all, Tatiana,' he murmured.

But he got up and cleared their plates first, poured them some more wine and studied the darkening waters of Darwin Harbour—which, as the locals were so fond of pointing out, was bigger than Sydney Harbour.

'When Leonie set up shop in Darwin a couple of years ago I was impressed by her skills and ideas. One thing led to another and we got into a relationship, but on the basis that we *both*,' he said significantly, 'had no wish for any further entanglement. She was passionate about her career and couldn't visualise herself as a wife and mother. Then, not long after our engagement, she decided to go back to America for some time and we parted.'

Tattie stared at him, wide-eyed.

'She didn't close her business but handed the reins to her chief assistant,' he continued. 'When she came back you and I were married, but she got in touch—ostensibly to show me some of the work she'd done overseas and the ideas she'd picked up. They were brilliant, and once more she started to work for Constantin as a freelance designer. However...' He paused and looked at her. 'Well, you know the state of our marriage, Tattie.'

'But why didn't you tell me this when I...when I—?'

'Delivered yourself of your ultimatums on our wedding night?' he drawled, and smiled faintly. 'I thought you had a point. I thought it would be less than right to force myself on you and I guess it seemed like a good idea to keep my options open. You did also give me your blessing.'

His last words fell into a pool of silence like stones dropping to the bottom of a well, and seemed to Tattie to contain an unmistakable undertone.

'Are you saying I forced you back into her arms?'

He grinned wickedly, but sobered almost immediately. 'Tattie, I know you're very young and quite naïve, but a year is a long time,' he said abruptly.

She sat back and drained her wine in a single swallow. 'I suppose so,' she replied at last, and could have kicked herself for feeling so particularly young and naïve at that moment—something she would normally have denied hotly. 'Uh—what happened then?' she asked.

'It became apparent that Leonie had revised her opinions on marriage and motherhood,' he said simply.

'How inconvenient for you,' she countered tartly.

His lips twitched. 'Another Beaufort thrust? Yes, it was,' he agreed, although blandly. 'But, whatever my sins are, Tattie—and I'm not trying to deny them—you would not have approved of Leonie Falconer in what one could only describe as "haggling mode". And, for your information, her true colours turned me right off.'

'She...she gave me to understand you'd become infatuated with me and that's why you'd cast her off. Was that true?' She gazed at him.

'Tattie, what you and I feel for each other is our own affair entirely,' he answered a little grimly. 'I have never discussed you with her or anyone else. Other than your mother,' he added drily.

'I see.'

'Talking of your mother...'

He paused and moved his shoulders in an impatient gesture, reminding Tattie of his ambivalence towards her mother—she was never quite sure whether he liked Natalie or viewed her as seriously nutty. 'Was that how you came to know ours was an arranged marriage?' he asked.

Tattie folded her hands in her lap and found an opportunity to refute the 'young and naïve' allegation, on some fronts anyway.

'I'm not quite stupid, you know, Alex,' she said finally. 'No, she never actually said it, but I know how her mind works.'

'So was it finding out about Leonie that convinced you?'

'It didn't help,' Tattie conceded. 'That, and the strong impression that you weren't in love with me.'

He favoured her with a darkly amused gaze. 'You thought you could tell?'

'I not only thought it, I could,' she stated stubbornly.

'What about you?'

Her lips parted and her eyes widened. 'What about me?'

'Your mother gave it to me as her considered opinion that you were in love with me.'

Tattie closed her eyes in frustration at her mother's

machinations, even if they happened to have hit the nail on the head...

'There was a bit of a crush,' she said, and tried to shrug fatalistically.

He grinned. 'Only a bit? So why did you do it, Tattie?'

Time to lay her cards on the table? she wondered with a little flicker of panic. What else could she do? None of what had just passed between them gave her the hope that Alex Constantin had fallen madly in love with her.

'I...' She gazed at the oil rig with its mantle of lights, then looked at her husband directly. 'I didn't know what else to do. Beaufort and Carnarvon were going downhill fast. Mum has always been like a displaced person out there and—' she sighed suddenly '—I didn't have the expertise or authority to run them myself, although I have this almost mystical tie to them and this perhaps ridiculously strong sense of...being a Beaufort.'

He said nothing for an age, and she watched his long fingers twirling the stem of his glass and his hooded eyes while she nerved herself to find that she was the object of his amusement.

But when he looked up at last there was no mirth in his gaze, no patronising disbelief. In fact he said quietly, 'We could be two of a kind, Tattie.'

'We could?'

He smiled absently. 'Both realists. Look, thanks for coming clean. However, if Beaufort and Carnarvon mean so much to you you're going to have to stay married to me.'

She swallowed something in her throat. 'Before I ask you why,' she said on a tremor, 'was that why you married *me*, Alex? To get them?'

He considered for a moment, then gestured wryly.

'They played a part, yes. I kept thinking of the—sorry!—mess they could get into with only you at the helm. It sort of…went against the grain with me, especially at a time when beef prices are going through the roof.'

'Oh.'

He looked at her intently for a long moment, at the gentle, slender lines of her figure beneath the pale rose silky knit of her top, the sweep of her dark hair against her throat and the shadows of her absurdly long lashes against her cheek as she looked down—in disappointment? he wondered.

'But I must tell you, Tattie, that I fully intended to make this a real marriage before you…said your little piece.'

Her lashes flew up and her deep blue eyes were suddenly surprisingly cynical. 'A marriage without love?'

'A marriage that would grow *into* love, respect and mutual expectations,' he said steadily. 'You may not think it can work but I've seen the evidence of it.'

'But—'

He overrode her. 'But living like brother and sister is not going to achieve it, Tattie. I hesitate to do this, but…' He paused. 'How you felt earlier on the couch is a prime reason to…go forward.'

'Alex—' She put her hands to her hot cheeks. 'I was in shock and horrified at what had happened to me. Don't you think that might have accounted for a lot of it?'

He smiled suddenly. 'Let's put it to the test again, now some of the shock and horror has receded.'

She stumbled up. 'No—I mean, no,' she stammered. 'Let's not.'

'What are you scared of, Tattie? How much you'll give yourself away?'

'Alex,' she said desperately, and dredged through to her soul to find an answer for him, 'I have one *very* good reason for not wanting to change our marriage at the moment. Maybe I'll tell you what it is one day, maybe I won't, but it's *there* and I can't help it.'

'Another mystery?' he said with considerable irony, and frowned.

'Another man?' he asked incredulously after a moment. 'But one who doesn't have the ability or the money to save Beaufort and Carnarvon for you—is *that* it, Tattie?'

She opened her mouth to pour supreme scorn on this supposition, then closed it, almost biting her tongue in two. 'There has been another woman in your life,' she pointed out.

'Who is he?'

'I didn't say that! I'm only... I don't see why you of all people should be so surprised if it were the case but...well, that's all I'm saying!'

'And do you honestly think I'd hand you over to another man to enjoy, along with two cattle stations I've rescued?'

There was something unusually grim in his dark eyes as they flickered over her.

'If you don't love me that can only be because you want them yourself or your macho Greek background is coming to the fore, Alex. Perhaps it's both,' she surmised, 'but either way it doesn't impress me.'

'Who the hell do you think you are, Tatiana?' he said softly, and added, 'I wouldn't trade on being a Beaufort too much with me, because I couldn't give a damn about that.' He stood up and reached for her.

Surprise was her downfall. It rooted her to the spot, it even opened her mouth for her, and he took advantage of it all to sweep her into his arms and bend his head to kiss her.

It was a hard, merciless kiss but, to her horror, it still ignited some of the fires he'd lit in her earlier in the afternoon. How could that *be*? she wondered helplessly, then knew—intuitively?—that sometimes between a man and a woman a release from their demons only came this way. But it didn't end that way...

When he had her helpless and aroused in his arms he lifted his head and, looking supremely macho, dark and dangerously attractive, said softly, 'You've been playing with matches for the last twelve months, Tatiana Beaufort. Don't be surprised when you get burnt.'

And he left her to stride away to his study, closing the door behind him.

'Pearling in northern Australia has a colourful history,' Tattie said, slowly and clearly.

She picked up a handful of lustrous free pearls and let them slip through her fingers into a velvet-lined porcelain bowl.

'"That elusive pearl, the one bigger, brighter and more beautiful than all the others"',' she quoted, 'has drawn men like a siren song, and they've described them as teardrops of the moon or a full moon rising...' She paused. 'Here at Constantin we produce the finest cultured Australian South Sea pearls, and I'd like to show you how.' She stopped and the camera clicked off.

'That was quite good, Mrs Constantin,' the director of the video said. 'Not too bad at all.'

But not good enough, Tattie said to herself, and looked around. It was two days after her attempted kid-

napping, but even more importantly two days after Alex
and she had come to a monumental misunderstanding.
So monumental that she'd forgotten, until reminded yesterday, that she'd agreed to, and even looked forward to,
making a video on the Constantin pearling operation, to
be played in their stores.

And she'd looked forward to it because there were
segments to be filmed at the actual pearl farms, as well
as in the luxurious Darwin showroom where she was
now, in a beautiful dusky-pink linen dress that shouted
couturier, and wearing her own pearls.

Trouble was, Alex was there too. Alex, leaning his
broad shoulders casually against a wall, out of the way
of the cameras but all the same—to her—an enemy in
a war, even if she wasn't sure what the precise nature
of the war was.

She'd hardly seen him over the past two days, but
when she had she'd been treated to cool uninterest.
She'd been told that their visit to Beaufort would have
to be postponed—he'd also forgotten about the video,
apparently, so it was a legitimate excuse, but she had no
doubt he would have made some other.

As for her feelings, they ranged from boiling indig-
nation through a certain sense of mystification and some
mortification to a nervous speculation about what she'd
brought on herself. She'd had time to reflect, and regret
bitterly, that she herself had driven him back into
Leonie's arms, even if she'd had little idea at the time
of what she was doing. All in all, she reflected, more
than enough under that dark gaze to become tongue-tied
and afflicted with stage fright.

'Uh…if I could just have a glass of water? Thank
you.'

'Tattie.' Alex straightened and came over to her. 'I

think you look a bit too solemn. You're supposed to be a gorgeous young woman full of the mystery and romanticism of pearls, alive and warm and vital—which you normally are.'

There was an embarrassed huffing and shuffling around the room as everyone avoided looking at anyone—apart from Tattie and Alex, whose gazes were locked.

'Alex…' Tattie licked her lips. 'This may sound crazy but I think I'd find it easier if you weren't here. You're making me self-conscious.'

'Uh…' The director interposed, and cleared his throat. 'That's not unusual. Acting is often easier in front of people you don't know. But I think you've made a good point, Mr Constantin. What we're striving for is exactly what you described.'

Everyone held their breath, including Tattie, but Alex looked amused, if anything, and with a shrug said, 'My dear Tattie, I would hate to discomfort you in any way, so I'll leave, but I'll meet you for lunch.' He left the showroom.

Why did that sound like a threat? Tattie wondered. His tone had been light and casual. Had she imagined the insolent flicker in his eyes in the last moment they'd rested on her? She didn't think so…

'When you're ready, Mrs Constantin,' the director said. 'Just take your time.'

Tattie turned away and took a deep breath. And she let her mind wander down the ages of pearl diving in the area since the 1850s. The hard-hat era of cumbersome brass helmets, the many Japanese divers who had made Broome and Thursday Island their home. The lovely but really remote bays and rivers of north-west Australia, the Northern Territory and far-north

Queensland that were so suitable for the farming of cultured pearls. All places where the scenery was spectacular and unspoilt, remote, tropical Australia in all its wild glory.

And she thought of the technology associated with cultured pearls. Diving for the wild shell, the delicate seeding operation, the care of the shells in those tropical waters as the oyster deposited layers of nacre around the minute seed to form a pearl.

She looked at the bowl of pearls beside her, all with an exquisite lustre or the quality of light being reflected from the surface of the pearl and at the same time refracted from within the nacre. At their different colours: white, white-pink, silver, gold, fancy and yellow. And their different shapes—circlé or baroque in this case. And she felt the magic of it all seep into her psyche…

She turned back to the cameras. 'I'm ready,' she said simply.

# CHAPTER FOUR

'REALLY red-hot sex liberates not only the body but also the mind—you should try it.'

Tattie faltered with her hand on a chair as she was about to sit down, and couldn't help but look round at the source of this advice. Alex had chosen the Darwin Sailing Club for lunch, a pleasant spot with tables outside under shady trees overlooking Fannie Bay and the flotilla of yachts anchored in it. It being a weekday, it wasn't crowded.

But there was a bearded, tattooed man with a Crocodile Dundee hat holding court a couple of tables away, and the advice had been offered to a woman companion who was looking singularly unaffected.

'Did you think that was directed at you?' Alex murmured as he pulled out her chair and waited politely for her to sit down.

'I didn't know what to think,' Tattie confessed.

He sat down opposite. 'Have you ever indulged in really red-hot sex?'

She bit her lip. 'I'm sure you have.'

'That doesn't answer the question.'

'Nor do I intend to.' Tattie fussed over the placement of her calfskin handbag that was dyed exactly to match her dress and added, 'I feel a little overdressed for the sailing club.'

'I wouldn't worry about it,' he drawled. 'I felt like being outdoors. And you don't have to look so embarrassed, we'll leave sex—of any kind—off the menu for the moment. As is your obvious preference.'

She shot him a fighting little look this time. 'Thank you. I'd appreciate it,' she said arctically. 'But if you've brought me to lunch in order to insult me—'

'Not at all,' he interrupted with his lips twisting. 'It came up out of the blue. How did the rest of the shoot go?'

She waited until their drinks had been placed—a glass of wine for her, a beer for him. 'I've been reliably informed by the director that I'm a natural once I get over my nerves. Not that I agree with him.' She wrinkled her nose. 'It wasn't really acting.'

'You must have managed to instil some more life into it than you were while I was there.'

'I did.'

'How?'

'Does it matter?'

'Yes. I'm really curious, Tattie.'

She eyed him, but could see only a genuine enquiry in his eyes. She sipped her wine and sat back. 'I love this part of the world, I love the Kimberley, as I've told you, and that's where a lot of the pearling history is, as well as the farms. And despite this being your company, Alex, it's…it's been fascinating to learn all about it, so I just made myself think about all that.'

'I'm glad something about your association with me has been fascinating. Shall we order?'

'Before we do that,' Tattie said in a swift undertone, 'I gather I'm in some kind of disgrace with you. Well, that's fine with me, and don't expect me to grovel, Alex! We know why we married each other, and in light of it I am still not prepared to be a dutiful little wife.'

'Or indulge in red-hot sex? It was getting pretty hot

the other day,' he said lazily. 'I got the distinct feeling you could no more help yourself than I…might have been able to.'

She looked around a little wildly. 'I can't believe you've chosen a place as public as this to have this kind of conversation with me!'

He raised a dark eyebrow and smiled satanically. 'Would you rather we were home alone?'

The most acute memories flooded Tattie, of that never-to-be-forgotten day, so that she had to drop her gaze and by a huge power of will block the vibes that were coming her way even with a table between them and the amount of discord that existed in the air.

In a light beige linen jacket, a cream shirt and khaki trousers, with his dark hair ruffled, Alex Constantin was the stuff to dream about. But the reality was turning out to be more sexy, more dangerously fascinating and less easy to handle than *she* had dreamt, and she'd been married to him for a year.

The knowledge awakened two things to be confused about. She might be in love with him, but would she ever be able to come up to what he needed in a woman? A twenty-one-year-old virgin who, thanks to her old-fashioned father and her mother's paranoia about fortune-hunters, had never really been let off the leash…

The other troubling point was how safe she felt with him in almost every other circumstance. As if there were suddenly two Alexes and she was unable to fuse them.

She clicked her tongue, shook her head, and said at random, 'I'd never seen so many beards and tattoos in a city until I came to Darwin. I guess it's the ''outback'' influence, because really, in the Northern Territory, even in the middle of Darwin, the outback is only a few miles down the Stuart Highway.'

He blinked, and said gravely, 'How true, Tattie!' Then he started to laugh. 'I take it you've given up?'

Her shoulders slumped. 'I'm not too sure what I'm fighting about,' she said honestly. 'It's all got very confusing.'

'It needn't be.'

'Alex…'

She stared at him and for a moment was unbearably tempted to let down her guard and place herself, body and soul, in his hands, but a sudden golden image of Leonie Falconer flashed before her mind's eye.

'Alex,' she said again, 'all my life I've been told what to do by people who believe they know what's best for me.' She shrugged. 'While I appreciate their love and concern, I need to make my own decisions now or I could become frozen in that mode. Do you—could you understand that?' she asked anxiously.

He stirred and broke his narrowed, intent study of her to look across the bay. 'Within limits,' he said at last. 'If you need more time—OK. Breaking up this marriage is not what I have in mind, however. But we don't have to make such heavy weather of it.' He smiled at her suddenly and nearly took her breath away. 'As soon as the video is finished we'll go to Beaufort.'

The next two weeks were busy and satisfying for Tattie.

She flew out to a pearl farm with Alex and the film crew and enjoyed not only filming the farming operation but also just being there. The Constantin mother ship was anchored in the Kimberley bay, with accommodation on it, and when they weren't filming she and Alex went fishing by dinghy up the Drysdale River.

Not as grand as the King George or the Berkeley, nevertheless the Drysdale had a timeless beauty of its own. Red cabbage-tree palms soared above the bushy, rock-strewn banks and the sand on the shores was pale gold. There were red-tailed black cockatoos with their large, lazy wingspan and their distinctive call. There were magnificent white-breasted sea eagles working the waters and a pair of brahminy kites with their white heads and tan feathers, always in the same spot, that she nicknamed George and Georgina.

There were crocodiles.

Often when they stopped to fish she looked at a rock or what appeared to be a log in the water, only to see it move and reveal itself as a knobbly, prehistoric crocodile. Or, as they were cruising along, what looked like a log on the bank would come to life and slide swiftly and silently into the water.

They caught barramundi, the holy grail of Australian fish, and her first catch was intensely exciting as she realised from the black-fringed flash of silver that leapt from the water what she had on her line. She refused any help from Alex, and after a magnificent fight managed to land it and collapse exhaustedly but delightedly with her catch—an eighty-centimetre fish.

One day they took a picnic lunch and steered the dinghy to the head of the river between rock walls that made her think of a Roman amphitheatre. It was as far as any boat could go anyway, before the river became a series of rapids and freshwater rock pools. There was a flat shelf along the bank and they climbed out and sat in the shade of the rock overhang to enjoy their picnic.

Tattie wore a green blouse and shorts over a blue bikini, a racy peaked cap with her hair tucked through the back, and sunglasses. It was a clear, warm day—they all were at this time of the year in this part of the world—and she stared up at the blue sky and breathed deeply.

Beyond Napier Broome Bay and the Drysdale River, the Timor Sea extended towards East and West Timor and Indonesia, and the equator wasn't that far away.

'It's like a last frontier, isn't it?' she said a little dreamily. 'So wild, untamed and wonderful.'

He nodded. 'I see what you mean.'

Tattie raised an eyebrow at him, because it seemed like an odd reply.

He poured two cups of tea from a Thermos flask. 'You really do love this part of the world—and it shows on the video now.' His lips quirked. 'You've also endeared yourself to everyone on the pearl farm with your infectious enthusiasm.'

She grinned impishly. 'It's nice to know I'm earning my keep. In a very small way.'

'Perhaps I ought to fly you up here on a regular basis. Staff morale is important in these out-of-the-way places, and with jobs still dangerous despite modern technology—like diving for the wild shells.'

She shivered suddenly. 'I was reading about King Sound the other day, and how many hard-hat divers it claimed with its treacherous deep-water drop-offs. I believe the area is still known as "The Graveyard"'.

'Pearling was a very hazardous occupation in those days. Decompression, drop-offs and squeezing were big problems, not to mention above-water catastrophes like cyclones that wiped out whole fleets before they had today's weather-forecasting technology. And all for buttons.'

'Buttons?'

'Uh-huh.' He unwrapped two slices of fruit cake and handed one to her to have with her tea. 'Mother-of-pearl for buttons was the mainstay of the pearling industry up here in those days. Gem pearls were very rare, but everyone needed buttons. Then plastic took over and the bottom fell out of the mother-of-pearl market. That's when the cultured-pearl industry was pioneered.'

Tattie was sitting cross-legged, enjoying her fruit cake. 'It's funny how the world turns. One door closes and another opens.'

Alex stood up and brushed his crumbs away. He had on a pair of khaki shorts and a grey T-shirt, which he now pulled over his head.

'Time for a swim. You know, Tattie, talking of things like that—how the world turns and earning your keep— there's another very good reason for staying married to me. You've taken to all this like a duck to water. You are an asset, and to have a wife who is as vitally interested in what one does as you are provides a very good framework for a marriage.'

She blinked behind her sunglasses.

'Take your mother, for example,' he said quietly. 'Word—gossip, possibly, but all the same—has it that she and your father did not have that in common, and you yourself told me she was like a displaced person at Beaufort. Did that help their marriage?'

'N-no, but…' She stopped and could only gaze up at him helplessly. This was the first time any discussion of their marriage had surfaced since lunch at the Darwin Sailing Club. And since that day Alex had gone back to being the Alex she'd known up until their wedding anniversary, apart from their brief and, she now realised, essentially chaste courtship.

Oh, yes, she'd conceded to herself several times lately, he had been able to make her tremble in his arms when he'd kissed her in those days, but that had been nothing to how he'd affected her when he'd really set his mind to it…

There was something else his words aroused in her. She would dearly love to prove to him that she was not just the trendy, social-butterfly daughter of her mother he might have taken her for. She would really like, she realised, to have the opportunity to prove her intelligence and substance to him, and taking a more active part in his business could be the way to do it.

But that was all he said or did. After waiting a moment for her reply he strolled over to the rock pool and lowered himself into the water with a groan.

'It's bloody cold,' he called to her.

'Go on, you're being a baby!' she responded, and stood up to strip off her blouse and shorts.

'Wait and see!' He disappeared under the water.

But she hesitated for a moment as she contemplated what she was up against now. No more red-hot sex? she thought with a tinge of humour that disappeared as fast as it had come. Logic instead, it seemed to her—sane, sensible realism. And, of course, he had a point—and one that struck right to the heart of her home—because he was also diabolically clever, Alex Constantin.

He was also right—the water was cold, so that she yelped as she slipped in and he laughed at her. But their trip back to the mother ship after they'd dried off and warmed themselves in the sun was quiet and swift.


'Tatiana, you're looking wonderful!'

Her mother had come round for coffee the first morning after Tattie's return.

'Thanks!'

'That light tan suits you,' Natalie said enthusiastically. 'Did you have a wonderful time? I believe the video is sensational.'

Tattie looked down at herself in filmy chalk-blue trousers and a matching loose over-blouse. 'Yes, I had a wonderful time, and everyone seems pleased with the video, but I don't know about sensational. I haven't seen the edited version yet.' She poured coffee from the percolator and sat down.

'I'm sure you're being modest,' Natalie said complacently. 'And I can't help wondering if that...sort of bloom you've got and the clothes you're wearing mean anything else?'

Tattie stared at her mother over the top of her cup, mystified. 'Bloom? Clothes?'

'As in needing a bit more space in your clothes. As in the stork being on the way, darling.'

Tattie put her cup down with a little clatter. 'Don't *you* start, Mum! I've been out in the open a lot, that's all. As for clothes, it gets hot up here, in case you haven't noticed, even at this time of the year!'

Natalie grimaced. 'Sorry! I just wondered. Who else has been bugging you—Alex?'

'His mother,' Tattie said darkly. 'She never lets an opportunity pass, but for your information, Mum, there is no problem; it's entirely up to Alex and me when we start a family.'

Natalie looked thoughtful. Then she said, 'I could always come back, of course.'

'What for? Come back from where?'

'Tatiana...' Natalie hesitated then took a deep breath. 'I'm getting married again. I hope this doesn't upset you; I hope you don't feel as if I'm deserting you or being unfaithful to your father's memory—although the truth of the matter is he...we...it wasn't an easy marriage...and I...I...' She stopped and looked, for once in her life, terrified.

Tattie got up swiftly and went to put her arms around

her mother. 'Mum,' she said softly, 'why are you scared of telling *me* this? I know how it was; I was there. And all I want for you is happiness!'

'Oh, Tattie,' Natalie said—one of the few times she'd shortened the name, 'there's a lot of Austin in you. Sometimes I see a glint of steel in you and it's made me wonder…but forget about that; I was so afraid you'd disapprove of me falling in love.'

'Tell me about it,' Tattie urged.

Ten minutes later she had it all. Natalie had fallen in love with a widowed artist who had been up in the Territory for the last six months painting Kakadu. They planned to live in Perth. There was such a glow about her mother as she spoke of the man in her life; Tattie saw a new and softer side to her that amazed her a little.

'But why would you feel as if you were deserting me?' she asked after they'd had a comfortable chat about this turn of events.

'Well, I brought you to Darwin, and I introduced you to Alex.' Natalie stopped and looked at Tattie a shade self-consciously. 'But it is all going well with you and Alex?' she asked intensely.

'Why shouldn't it be?' Tattie replied with what she hoped was just the right amount of unconcern.

'I…' Natalie hesitated and sighed. 'You know that glint of steel you inherited from your father that I mentioned earlier? I sometimes can't help wondering if you didn't have your own agenda for Alex Constantin, Tatiana.'

Tattie knew suddenly—inexplicably, but knew all the same—that she couldn't and didn't want to fence with her mother any longer. Perhaps it had something to do with this new, softer Natalie, or perhaps for the first time she felt on an equal footing with her.

'I did,' she said, and told her mother the truth about her marriage for the first time.

'Now I feel really terrible,' Natalie pronounced. 'Now I know I can't leave you!'

'Nonsense,' Tattie said, but affectionately. 'I went into it with my eyes open. No amount of matchmaking would have pushed me where I didn't want or didn't need to go, Mum. So you may go to Perth and start your new life with my blessing! It's not as if it's the other side of the world anyway.'

'Talk about role reversal!' Her mother looked at her ruefully.

'All the same, I'm so happy for you,' Tattie said softly. 'When do I get to meet him?'

Natalie sat back, as if relieved of a huge burden. 'Tomorrow night, if you and Alex would like to come to dinner.' She sat up suddenly. 'About Alex...surely I could—'

'Mum,' Tattie said firmly, 'you leave Alex to me—I mean that,' she warned.

Natalie blinked a couple of times. 'You've got even more of Austin in you than I thought. I wonder if Alex realises what he's up against?'

And for some reason they laughed quietly together.

Tattie was not so sanguine when she was alone, however.

So far as she could see Alex held all the cards and was determined to use them. Whilst she was holding out for him to fall madly in love with her but was seriously concerned that she might not be woman enough for him if he did.

She grimaced, shook her head and wondered if she was mad...

\*   \*   \*

'Well, well,' Alex said that night when she told him about her mother's impending marriage.

'What does that mean?' Tattie enquired, suddenly prepared to defend her mother to the death. 'I don't think I've ever seen her so happy.'

Alex threw his jacket over the back of a chair, pulled off his tie and pushed up his shirtsleeves. He'd been in a series of conferences all day, he'd told her, and he wasn't looking relaxed.

'It means what it says,' he replied. 'Surprise—because I thought her life revolved around you, I guess.'

'You don't like her,' Tattie stated tautly.

'When you bargain with someone over their daughter, liking them is not an emotion that comes into play. I suppose I don't relate to her, that's all.'

'She can be...' Tattie started again. 'She really thought it was best for me.'

'She certainly protected your interests like a tigress.' He looked around the apartment reminiscently.

Tattie swallowed awkwardly. 'I didn't know about that until it was a *fait accompli*.'

'I know. I mightn't have married you otherwise.' He moved across to the bar and poured himself a Scotch. 'Want one?'

'No, thank you.' She sank onto the cream settee and pulled a pewter cushion into her lap to hug. 'Sorry to be repetitious—but what does *that* mean?'

Alex finished mixing his drink and cast himself down in an armchair. 'A mother out to get all she can for her daughter is one thing. A wife out to get all she can from her husband is another.'

'Agreed,' Tattie said coolly. 'But I was bringing you two cattle stations.'

'That remains to be seen. The marriage contract stipulates that, unless by mutual consent, what is yours remains yours and what is mine remains mine, with our children being the beneficiaries of our estates.'

'All the same, don't you feel you might have got your morals a little twisted, Alex?'

He put his drink down on a side-table and contemplated her out of cynical dark eyes. 'I'll tell you how I feel, Tattie—sick and tired of all this. I'll tell you what I'd like to do. Have a nice, relaxing meal, perhaps a stroll through the park, and then I'd like to bring my wife home and take her to bed.'

Tattie stared at him over the top of the cushion with her lips parted.

'I'll tell you something else,' he went on drily. 'You would feel much less aggressive, combative and scratchy if you allowed me to do that.'

'Scratchy?' It came out hoarsely.

'As in wanting to scratch my eyes out over an innocent remark about your mother,' he elucidated.

Tattie cast the cushion aside and stood up. 'You're wrong—I'd rather die—'

'No, you wouldn't.' He stood up swiftly and reached for her. 'But if you want to go on playing girlish games with me, how about this one?'

She refused to allow herself the indignity of trying to struggle out of his arms. But her eyes were bright with anger at his gibe—because it had hit home, no doubt exactly as he'd intended. What he didn't know was that it had also ignited a spark within her, fast becoming a flame of desire—to show the world, Leonie Falconer and particularly Alex Constantin that she was not to be underestimated in any way but in this regard especially.

'Girlish?' she breathed. 'Perhaps that's one of the

areas of me that's a closed book to you, Alex? So let me show you otherwise.'

She slipped her hands around his neck and offered him her mouth at the same time as she moved her body sensuously against his. She was still wearing the filmy chalk-blue outfit, so there was not a lot between her skin and the hard, warm feel of his body against hers.

Nor did she allow herself to rush or be rushed. When his mouth came down hard on hers she resisted, and went to trail a line of butterfly kisses down his throat. And she opened a few more buttons of his shirt so she could slide her hands beneath it and smooth the skin of his shoulders.

'Mmm...nice,' she said huskily, and opened her blue eyes at him.

'Tattie...' He said her name in a low growl and his eyes were hard but hot.

'Perhaps you should call me Tatiana,' she suggested impishly. 'I always know you're cross with me when you do that. Although why you should be cross is a bit of a mystery.'

'Tattie...you're playing with fire,' he warned.

'You may kiss me now, Alex,' she replied.

He held himself in check for one long, tense moment, then he did so, and she gave herself up to his mouth and his hands on her, sure and devastatingly adept at seeking her most sensitive areas.

So when she discovered herself back on the couch, but in his arms this time, and minus the bottom half of her outfit, her nipples were aching in the most divine way, her mouth was bruised and she was shivering with desire, uncaring if she'd lit a fire she now had no control over.

Because all her senses were alive and drinking in Alex

Constantin: the rough feel of the end-of-the-day stubble on his jaw against the smoothness of her skin; the hard strength of his body; the heat of his desire. So much so, she was ready to surrender her virginity to him, even though she'd started this as a lesson. How ironic, she thought as he slipped her shirt off and looked down at the pale blue bra that matched her briefs.

But there was a serpent in paradise. And the irony of *that* was—she had introduced it.

He slid his fingers between her thighs, then looked into her eyes. 'So,' he said barely audibly, 'my wife may not be the virgin I was promised. Who is he, Tattie?'

If someone had thrown a bucket of cold water over her the effect could not have been more punishing. She gasped and sat upright incredulously. 'That was *not* in the marriage contract!' she denied.

A cool, absent smile twisted his lips. 'It was what I was given to understand, and quite important in this kind of marriage.'

'What do you mean?' she asked in a deadly undertone.

He shrugged. 'In the context of being able to mould you into a wife who would suit me.'

Tattie sprang off the couch with her hair flying like rough black silk. 'I knew it,' she fumed. 'Don't think this has come as any surprise to me—I hate it!'

She planted her hands on her hips, then made the mistake of looking down at herself, clad only in three triangles of pale blue silk. She closed her eyes briefly, and snatched her shirt and pulled it on. Then she looked around for the other half of her outfit and, with as much dignity as possible, fished her trousers out from beneath the coffee-table. But it was hard to maintain a lot of dignity as she stood on one leg, then the other, and wriggled into them.

It was just as well that her sense of outrage was enormous, and once again she was able to plant her hands on her hips, this time fully dressed, if slightly awry.

Alex remained sprawled out on the settee and eyed her as he ran his hand through his hair and fingered his jaw. 'Hate what?' he enquired gravely, but in a way that barely hid a restrained spark of humour. 'There didn't seem to be an awful lot of hate going on just now.'

'Your Greek background,' she said fiercely, 'and this whole business of arranged marriages to virgins you can *mould* into suitable wives!'

'Oh, that. What about your own mother, who didn't seem to think it was such a bad idea?'

'She might have thought she was arranging a highly suitable marriage for me, but *I* never had any intention of being a virgin bride you could *train* to suit your tastes.'

He grimaced. 'Are you a virgin, Tattie?'

'Why? Are you having doubts now that I might be? A pity, because it's something you may be destined never to know.'

He folded his arms. 'That is throwing down the gauntlet, Tattie.'

'Oh!' She ground her teeth.

'On the other hand, let's forget about moulding, training and all that—'

'*You* brought it up!'

'Perhaps I was taken by surprise.' He raised his eyebrows quizzically. 'Uh—on the other hand, how badly do you want me to go on rescuing Beaufort?'

'What…what do you mean?'

'I mean it's come to the stage where a significant cash

inflow is required. Of course you could do it yourself—
if you sold Carnarvon.'

Something clicked into place in Tattie's mind, something he'd said to her a couple of weeks ago, but in the
heat of *that* moment she'd forgotten to query it.
Something about not being able to run the stations without him, anyway...

She sat down on the coffee-table unexpectedly. 'Sold
Carnarvon?'

'You have plenty of assets, Tattie, but not a lot of
cash.'

'But...I thought beef prices were going through the
roof.'

'They are. Your beef, however, is thinly spread over
two huge stations in a way that's going to require a
massive mustering operation, the cost of which alone
will eat away most of your profits this year.'

'I know that. We've been through this before, Alex.'
She swallowed. 'I told you that's what I was very much
afraid of. There hasn't been a proper muster for a couple
of years and a lot of the stock has gone feral. You
said—'

'Tattie,' he interrupted, 'what I've done for you is
this: during the last dry we mustered what we could—
not a lot, but all the same—and with the proceeds spent
the wet season improving as much of the facilities as we
could. The bores, yards, equipment, et cetera. But what
we were not able to do during the wet season was im-
prove the roads, particularly on Carnarvon, which have
since suffered some bad wash-aways during the last wet.
It's almost impossible to get a road train through there
now, Tattie.'

She was silent, counting the cost of it mentally.

'On top of that,' he continued, 'you know what a big

muster means. Extra ringers and horses, helicopters for the really difficult terrain and the wilder stock, freight costs and all the rest.'

'So—this may sound like a silly question,' she said at last, and looked anxious, 'but where are we at? Am I in hock to you already?'

'A new road into Carnarvon would put you there.'

'I'm sure I could get a loan.' She bit her lip, then suddenly looked around the apartment. 'Or I could give you this! I haven't really done anything to earn it.'

'You could do that.' He shrugged. 'Or you could form a real partnership with me.' He looked at her significantly.

'I got the impression you might not want me, assuming I was "soiled goods", Alex.'

'I didn't say that,' he countered. 'Although you would have to put away any aspirations you had towards having another man in your life.'

'Like you put away Leonie Falconer, and whoever her replacements might be?' she asked innocently.

He stood up. 'Those are my terms, Tattie. Take it or leave it. In the meantime, the dry season is progressing and there's a strong chance Carnarvon won't get mustered this year.' He reached for his jacket and slipped it on.

'Where are you going?'

He looked at her mockingly. 'Out.'

# CHAPTER FIVE

NOR had he come home that night, Tattie discovered the next morning.

Of course there was the house at Brinkin, a new home right on Casuarina Beach, a home with big grounds to bring up children in, ironically.

So it didn't automatically follow that she might have driven him back into Leonie's arms, she reasoned, but shivered all the same.

Then she got a call from her father-in-law, who asked if he could come and have a cup of coffee with her. Of course, she told him, but it was an unusual enough request to make her frown at the phone before she put it down, and to wonder what it was all about.

More pressure to start a family? Little did George know...

But she dressed with care in a three-quarter-length denim skirt and a cap-sleeved fine white rib-knit top, tucked in, a patent turquoise belt around her waist and turquoise mules on her feet. She also took pains to be perfectly groomed and her hair gleamed with vitality.

'Pretty as a picture!' George Constantin beamed at her. He sniffed the air. 'And your coffee smells gorgeous!'

Tattie thanked him and reflected that if the advice about looking at a girl's mother before you married her held good for a man's father, any wife of Alex Constantin would be reassured. George Constantin was grey now, but still reminiscent of his son in his tall, only slightly stooped bearing, still, really, a fine figure of a man. And his manners were courtly, he had a nice sense of humour and a way of making you feel at ease.

Well, she amended as she poured the coffee and offered him a plate of homemade shortbread, not as at ease as he usually made her feel.

'Irina is not with you today, George?' She sat down and took her own piece of shortbread.

'Sadly not, Tatiana. Her hip is playing up a little—we may have to consider a replacement soon, if only I can persuade her out of her fear of hospitals. This is delicious!' He helped himself to another biscuit. 'Did you make it?'

'I was hoping you wouldn't ask me that.' Tattie wrinkled her nose. 'I cannot tell a lie! My cleaning lady, who often helps me out with dinner parties, also keeps me in a constant supply of goodies like these. She's a gem. But I'm sorry to hear about Irina. Is there anything I can do?'

George waved a hand. 'No, thank you, my dear, but it's so kind of you to offer. By the way, I ran into Alex last night.'

'Oh.' Tattie went still for a moment.

'Mmm,' her father-in-law said, and hesitated for a long moment. 'And that's why I wanted to see you today, Tattie,' he finished.

She stared at him. 'Where…did you run into him?'

'In a pub. There was a Bledisloe Cup match on last night—rugby union, between the Wallabies and the All Blacks,' he explained, and looked mischievous. 'I have some mates I always watch those games with, have a few beers and so on, but Irina hates me filling the house with them so…' He shrugged.

Tattie smiled understandingly on several fronts.

Despite the millions he'd made, George was renowned in Darwin for his common touch. And her mother-in-law was exceptionally house-proud as well as a teeto-taller.

'But there was Alex,' George went on, 'alone—don't think he even knew the game was on—and—'

'Not in a very good mood,' Tattie finished quietly.

A keen dark glance came her way, although George said, 'Perhaps, although he joined in and appeared to enjoy the game. It's just that I know Alex well; this was rather uncharacteristic and I could tell he had something on his mind, Tattie. But if this is just a little "domestic", my dear, tell me to mind my own business and I'll go home. Not until I've finished my excellent coffee, though!'

Tattie thought for a bit as she stirred her own coffee until it was about to overflow. 'You wouldn't have come here if that's all you thought it was, would you?' she said eventually.

George shrugged. 'No. You see, I wondered—I know this sounds crazy—but I wondered how well you know Alex, Tattie?'

She blinked.

'I've even wondered if this marriage is the fairy tale made in heaven it outwardly appears to be.' He gazed at her soberly.

'How...how did you guess?' she whispered, then closed her eyes as she realised she'd given herself away completely.

'Call me an old fool,' he said slowly, 'but not once have I ever seen a sign of spiritual closeness between you two. I've seen affection and, yes, you laugh to-gether, but I've never seen any spark of real physical tension between you, and I have never seen him look at

you the way we men look at the women we desire. For
that matter, the same goes for you, Tattie.'

'What did you expect?' Tattie heard herself ask huskily. 'He was never in love with me. Even I realised
that. It was all arranged, and forgive me, George, but I
can't believe you and Irina didn't have something to do
with that.'

'As well as Natalie, your mother.'

'At least my mother thought I was in love with him.'

'Were you?' George asked gently.

Tattie looked away and refused to reply.

'My marriage to Irina was an arranged one,' he said
slowly. 'But, while I may slip out to watch rugby with
the boys, we couldn't be closer.'

'That's…lovely, but…' She spread her hands helplessly. 'How many years did it take to get that way?'

He stirred. 'A good question. You're saying a year is
not a very long time? True. But at least you have to
make a start.'

Tattie frowned at him. 'Has Alex been talking to
you?' she asked incredulously.

George shook his head ruefully. 'Alex has been a perfect son in many respects, but he's always gone his own
way—no, he would never do that. And it was only by
accident that I discovered something not even his mother
has ever known. Something that just might help you to
understand him better, my dear Tatiana.'

Tattie looked at him wide-eyed.

'There was a girl once; Flora Simpson was her name.
She and Alex were very much in love. But she was
married, and she went back to her husband. You know
how oysters coat an irritant with a layer of nacre? That's
what happened to Alex; he acquired a hard, protective
shell after that.'

'You knew this but you still connived at an arranged marriage for Alex with me?' Tattie asked after it had all sunk in. 'George, forgive me again, but you…your intuition about Alex and me has been astonishingly accurate, but you can't think much of women if you could do that—' She stopped abruptly.

'Do that to you, Tattie?' he said softly.

'I…' She bit her lip.

'If you love him like that, Tattie,' George went on, his dark eyes full of compassion that made her want to burst into tears, 'isn't he worth fighting for?'

'He may *never* forget her!'

'He might think that, but life goes on; things change,' George said wisely. 'Do you have a choice, though?'

That afternoon Tattie flew by commercial airline across the border to Kununurra, Western Australia, and from there she chartered a light plane to take her to Beaufort.

She'd left a note for Alex and she'd postponed her dinner with her mother and the man Natalie planned to marry. She'd also requested Alex not to follow her for a couple of days, if he was so minded, saying she needed a bit of time on her own.

It was the head stockman's wife, Marie, who met her at the airstrip and drove her up to the homestead, apologising all the way for not having had time to spruce the place up.

'Don't worry about it,' Tattie told her lightly. 'I haven't come to check for dust under the beds and I brought some supplies from Kununurra. But could you ask Jim if I can have a horse tomorrow and, if he has the time to show me around, I'd like to see all the improvements that have been made lately?'

Marie agreed to that enthusiastically and then reluctantly, as if she could sense Tattie needed to be alone but didn't approve, left her.

In fact the homestead was in pretty good order, and once the generator was going Tattie had power and hot water. And, since she'd lived in the rambling house on and off all her life, it held no terrors for her to be there alone.

She built up a fire in the lounge, cooked herself scrambled eggs and ate them in front of the fire. It was a huge room, and there were pictures of Beaufort ancestors—one of whom had been a premier of Western Australia—on the walls. But Natalie's was the latest influence on the homestead. Accordingly—and Tattie thought ruefully back to her mother's ongoing battles with her father over this—many renovations had been made and it had a sense of style.

There were decent bathrooms, the kitchen was practical and modern, there were good beds and fine linen and some lovely furniture.

All the same, she thought as the fire flickered and cast leaping shadows—and this might have frightened her mother—you could never forget how remote you were. You might install air-conditioning but you only had to step outside to encounter the sometimes savage heat, the flies, the torrential downpours of the wet season.

You didn't have to go far at all from the homestead to find yourself in a wilderness where rivers cut deep gorges into the land, where billabongs supported delicately coloured water lilies, paperbark trees, buffalo grass that floated on the water and an amazing array of bird life. You could ride to a burnt-sienna rocky outcrop in a sea of low olive-green scrub, and you could sit on the top beneath a huge sky and feel the heartbeat of a timeless, ancient land as you observed what made this country so special to its traditional owners.

At least she could, she mused, as her father had taught her to appreciate it, as his father had taught him. She could identify a jacana, a tiny bird that hopped about the water-lily pads on feet as long as its body, and all the birds on the billabongs. Lizards, monitors, even snakes fascinated her, as did the little rock wallabies, the wombats and big red kangaroos she sometimes saw.

What she hadn't absorbed so thoroughly—and this was partly due to her mother's wish to keep her as lady-like as possible—were the trials and tribulations of running cattle on this land so that they both flourished.

And that was why she'd willingly lived away from Beaufort for a year now, to try to glean the know-how she lacked from Alex. She'd even enjoyed herself, for the most part, but she knew now that she'd been incredibly naïve.

Was it worse to know why Alex was the way he was? she asked herself with her head resting back and her feet up on a footstool as she stared at the ceiling. How did it help in the equation she was faced with now? The stark knowledge right out in the open that if she wanted his help to save her heritage a proper marriage was what was required of her in exchange.

Why had she closed her mind to the reality that it would have to come to this? she wondered dismally. Why had she allowed herself to play with silly ultimatums, such as she would only consummate this marriage if she knew Alex was madly in love with her?

She closed her eyes and pressed her cheek against the smooth plum velvet of the wing chair. Because she had been too young and too foolhardy to know what she was getting herself into, she answered herself. Because she *had* secretly believed she could make him fall in love with her…

Only now to discover she'd never had a chance.

So, what about the question George had posed? She hadn't answered; she'd only wanted the embarrassment of it all to end as soon as possible. She'd tried to tell herself she wasn't even sure what he'd meant. Did she have a choice regarding Beaufort and Carnarvon?

But all the time a sinking certainty had presented itself—if she was that much in love with his son, would leaving him make it stop?

Was she that much in love with Alex? she wondered suddenly. She'd lived with him like a sister for a year. How had she done that if she was so madly in love with him?

Another sinking certainty presented itself to her—he had made it impossible for her to be any other way than sisterly. But things had changed, hadn't they? she reminded herself. Things had got to a stage where she only had to be in the same room as him to be conscious of him in a most unsisterly way…

And suddenly she was crying at the terrible sadness of it all. Of Alex loving a woman he couldn't have, of herself dying to be truly loved by him.

She took herself to bed eventually and woke up with her mind clearer.

Tatiana Constantin née Beaufort was a new person as of today. Gone was the social butterfly, gone was the naïve girl who'd thought she could make a very experienced man fall in love with her. Gone was the innocent, the *ingénue*. And from today she would be assessing how she could save Beaufort and Carnarvon without having to spend the rest of her life married to a man who couldn't love her.

'So, Jim.' Tattie took her hat off and wiped her brow as she sat on a well-mannered brown mare. 'Beaufort looks to be in pretty good shape…the new yards and loading ramp, the six-mile bore et cetera—but what about Carnarvon?'

It was a clear blue day, the temperature was thirty degrees and the dust from a mob of cattle being moved to the main holding yards hung in the air. Air that was alive with whistles and hoofbeats, moos, the occasional yelp of a cattle dog—and lots of sticky little flies.

'Miss Tattie,' Jim said, 'things aren't so good over there, mate.'

He was dry and wiry, and he'd known her since she was ten. He looked into the far blue yonder. Beaufort and Carnarvon were adjoined, but their common border was one of extremely rough terrain for the most part, almost impenetrable rock-strewn gullies and sheer cliffs. Which meant a long way round getting between the two stations.

'The last wet played havoc with the main road in, and the stock last time I did a recce was all gone bush and needs a damn good weeding out anyway,' he continued laconically.

She raised an eyebrow at him.

'Because Carnarvon is a lot rougher country than Beaufort generally, it's always been a problem to get rid of the shorthorn influence. There are a lot of wild scrubber bulls lurking in them gullies—used to annoy the hell out of your dad, may he rest in peace.'

'Jim,' Tattie said slowly, 'would it be fair to say Carnarvon is becoming—unviable?'

'As is, sure,' he responded. 'But I thought… I mean Alex…' He stopped and looked at her. 'What I mean is, with a bit of work and the way beef prices are going,

Carnarvon could be made to pay its way. Your dad would never have parted with it and—'

'I know,' Tattie interrupted. 'It was just a thought.'

'The last time he was here on his own,' Jim said thoughtfully, 'Alex, I mean—we flew over the boundary and we found one spot where he thought you could make a road to join 'em up. I tell you what, Miss Tattie, it would make both of 'em a hell of a lot more viable. If we could get that stock over here we could have one main operation rather than two separate ones. But it would take a bit of dosh to build that road.'

It stuck in Tattie's throat, fortunately, the frustrated urge to enquire at large why her husband had seen fit not to share this news with her. But perhaps those were the ideas he'd mentioned to her? And would have confided to her if she'd been a good little wife in *all* respects?

Then Jim looked up and shaded his eyes at the same time as Tattie became aware of a buzzing above.

'Speak of the devil,' he said.

'That's Alex?' she asked incredulously as a light plane flew over them.

'Sure is. Recognise that beaut little bird anywhere!'

'So I'll thank you never to do that again, Tattie,' her husband said grimly.

She'd ridden back to the homestead to arrive just as Marie had dropped him off from the airstrip. And she supposed she should be grateful that he'd waited until they were inside and alone before he'd commenced to tear strips off her for allowing him to wonder whether she'd been kidnapped again.

'But I left you a note!' she protested.

'You should be more careful with your notes in future.

It fell down behind the hall table and I only found it because I dropped my car keys—three hours after you'd apparently disappeared off the face of the earth. But that's not all.'

'I...I—'

He overrode her. 'Tattie, I never wanted to scare the daylights out of you but, since it—almost—happened once, you need to adopt a bit of caution. Buzzing off on your own without any consultation is not on, do you *understand*? Surely you're mature enough for that?'

Tattie breathed in and exhaled deliberately. It didn't help. Nothing helped her in this confrontation with her tall, angry husband. And it mysteriously added fuel to the fire because he so much looked the part of a cattleman, lean and tough in jeans and a bush shirt, whereas she felt like a girl desperately trying to *play* a part.

'What's the problem, Alex?' she said. 'The next time someone tries to kidnap me you could tell them to go ahead, because I'm not the wife you want, am I? It could even solve a few problems.'

'What the hell are you talking about?' he ground out.

Tears were starting to create dark rivulets down her dusty cheeks and she wiped her nose on the back of her hand. 'I'm talking about not being Flora Simpson, or whatever her name is. I'm talking about— Alex—' She broke off on a breath and winced as he took her by the shoulders and his fingers dug in hard.

'Who...?' He didn't finish, but stared down at her with such a blaze of anger in his eyes she literally felt herself shrink beneath his hands. Then he blinked and seemed to get himself under better control. 'My father?'

She swallowed, and would have given anything to keep her mouth shut.

'It had to be,' he said and swore.

'I think he was only trying to help,' Tattie offered tentatively.

'When was this?'

She told him haltingly.

'So that's why you scuttled home to Beaufort, Tattie?'

All the bravado of a few moments ago had drained out of Tattie, but she couldn't let this pass entirely. 'You had a bit to do with it yourself, Alex.'

He stared down at her searchingly, then seemed to make a decision. 'All right, go and wash your face and I'll make us a drink. It is lunch time.'

'Perhaps we should eat rather than drink?'

He smiled slightly. 'I'll see what I can do. Off you go.'

When she got back it was to find that he'd made some substantial ham sandwiches and poured them each a gin and tonic.

And he waited until she'd had a sandwich and sipped her drink before he said, 'You'd better tell me the whole story.'

She didn't, of course, but she offered him the gist of his father's concern.

He looked heavenwards and commented bitterly on the trials of being an only son. Then he looked at her directly and said, 'That was six years ago, Tattie, and I sent Flora Simpson back to her husband when I discovered she liked to have her cake and eat it.'

Tattie looked at him wide-eyed.

'I am not pining for her,' he added, and shook his head in a rather weary disclaimer. 'I got over it all years ago.'

'So why does your father think…?'

He grimaced. 'They're both desperate for a grandchild.'

Tattie frowned, but decided to hold her peace—for the time being anyway. 'Why didn't you tell me about the possibility of a road between the two stations?'

'That's a switch of topics! Not that a break from the tortured course of this marriage isn't welcome... Uh, it would cost, that's why. I think it would be worth it in the long run but—'

'It brings us right back to the tortured course of this marriage, doesn't it?' Tattie suggested sweetly, then sat back, suddenly mentally exhausted.

Alex watched her for a long moment—the way she sipped her gin and tonic, then put it down as if she wasn't enjoying it at all, the way her hands clasped then unclasped in her lap, the shadows he suddenly noticed beneath her eyes. More vulnerable, he thought, than he'd ever seen her...

'Let's take a break,' he said suddenly.

She looked a question at him.

'Would you like me to fly you over the area where I think a road is a possibility this afternoon?'

There was no mistaking the sudden eagerness in her eyes, but then her shoulders slumped. 'I couldn't afford it so it may be better not to get too worked up about the idea. Alex—' she took a deep breath '—I really came here, and I intend to stay here, to try to work out a way I can run at least Beaufort without having to depend on you in any way.'

'It means that much to you?' he said slowly.

No, *you* mean too much to me for me to put myself through a loveless marriage to you, and I haven't discounted the Flora Simpson scenario yet, she answered him in her mind.

She said instead, 'I thought it was about time I...got

a bit mature about all this.' The faintest smile lit her blue eyes. 'I've made quite a few mistakes, obviously—'

'The biggest being marrying me?'

'As it's turned out, yes. So—'

'You really thought a year with me would give you the expertise you lacked?' he asked probingly.

'Obviously,' Tattie said again. 'Now I know otherwise there's only one thing for me to do, and that's get stuck into it myself.'

Alex sat back and continued to watch her as she tilted her chin Beaufort-style, and resolutely squared her shoulders. And it came to him that whatever he felt for Tatiana Beaufort he would not rest easy until he'd discovered what made her tick. He'd let her have her way for a year, he reflected. Then he'd applied a bit of pressure to get their marriage going, only to come to this.

So what if he used more subtle measures? he mused. Not such a hardship, really. While it was her fighting spirit he found fascinating, she was also rather gorgeous. And, he reflected, there was the curious fact that barely two days ago her trim little body had been warm and pliant and as sexy as hell in his arms—but now this.

'What are you thinking?' She broke into his reverie, looking slightly nervous.

He shrugged. 'I was wondering if I could give you a crash course in cattle-station management, seeing you're so determined to leave me,' he said casually. 'I have the next week free.'

Her long dark lashes fluttered and her blue eyes were wide and startled. 'Just like that? I mean…with no strings attached?'

It passed through his mind to think—Got you, Tattie Beaufort!—only to wonder immediately what kind of a bastard he was. But he reminded himself that it had al-

ways been her intention to use him; OK, she might have
been very young and not known what she was getting
herself into, but all the same...

'No strings attached. And no guarantees I'll be successful. But we can try.'

'Oh, thank you!' she breathed, looking suddenly radiant. 'Can we start now, today?'

Another thought crossed Alex Constantin's mind.
What effect would it have on him were she to look as
radiant about *him* rather than a damn cattle station? But
he dismissed it. 'Sure. I'll give you an aerial tour of
Carnarvon this afternoon, so you know just what you're
up against.'

But it was rather a glum Tattie who sat down to dinner
with him that night. She'd cooked them steak, egg and
chips, and they'd had to push a lot of paperwork aside
to be able to eat at the dining-room table.

She'd seen for herself the diabolical state of the main
road into Carnarvon, the way the stock was thinly spread
over tortuous country, the shorthorn influence that they'd
been able to eradicate from Beaufort in favour of
Brahmin or Brahmin-cross cattle. He'd taken her through
the bookwork Jim had provided, and she was looking
exhausted again.

'Enough of this,' Alex said when she went to look at
the paperwork again after they'd eaten. 'You relax; I'll
make the coffee.'

But when he came back with it she was asleep in the
wing chair.

He looked down at her for a long time. At the absurdly
long lashes lying on her cheeks, at the twisted grace of
her lithe body—and he wondered again at what he

thought he was doing in the moment before he picked her up gently and carried her to bed.

Breakfast was steak again, cooked this time by Alex.

'Sorry you had to put me to bed,' Tattie said as she looked at her steak and remembered waking up in her shirt and briefs, having been divested of her jeans. 'I must have been out like a light.'

'You were. So I thought we might take it easy today. Are there any special places on Beaufort we could ride to?'

She forgot about the indignity of being partially undressed and looked at him eagerly. 'There's my favourite billabong; it's only about an hour's ride away.'

'Should we take a picnic?'

'I'd love to!' She picked up her knife and fork and looked much more enthusiastic about her breakfast. 'I'm sure Jim will have a horse for you.'

Jim did, a raking chestnut gelding that eyed Alex and gave every indication of taking exception to his weight on its back. Five minutes later, though, it was behaving itself impeccably.

Tattie tipped her hat to Alex. 'Didn't take you long to let him know who's the boss!'

He looked over to her seated on her mare. 'Best to get it over and done with in my opinion.'

'In more walks of life than one,' Tattie said mischievously.

'But not with you, Tattie,' he responded. 'Shall we go?'

'Follow me!'

Several hours later they were eating their picnic lunch beside the billabong and Tattie was pointing out the wonders of it all to him. 'I've been coming here since I was six,' she told him, 'on my first pony. It was also the year I got a puppy, now I come to think of it. This darling little blue heeler Dad found for me.'

'What happened to him?'

'He went to the great hunting ground in the sky a bit prematurely.' She looked sad.

'Did you get another one?'

'No. Dad wanted me to but I was away at boarding-school most of the time so there didn't seem much point.'

'So…' He leant back on his elbow. 'You got on pretty well with your father?'

She grimaced. 'Yes, but not always. I know he would have loved to have a son, but Mum fought tooth and nail not to have him turn me into a son by proxy, so I often felt like the meat in a sandwich.' She shrugged. 'I often wonder if life wouldn't have been easier if she'd let him have his way—he turned out to be extremely strict with me as a daughter.'

'I think he'd be very proud of you as a daughter.'

'Do you? Why?' Tattie asked interestedly.

'You're feisty, you're interesting, most people light up when you're around and—you're lovely.'

Tattie nearly dropped her tin mug and splashed hot tea all over her jeans.

'I've surprised you,' he murmured.

'A bit,' she conceded. 'I guess because I somehow manage to be—all froth and bubble when I'm with you.'

He looked amused. 'If I thought that at first, I've revised my opinions. And you have been—other things with me.'

She coloured, but said valiantly, 'With disastrous consequences, Alex. I didn't think you approved at all!'

'Perhaps I'm having trouble putting my finger on the real Tattie Beaufort,' he said after a moment. 'Not that it's a problem now.'

'No,' she said slowly, and stood up to begin putting the picnic things together. 'Your parents…' She paused and looked at him with a comically rueful expression.

'Not to mention your mother, Tattie.' He sat up. 'But we married each other, not them, so it's our business.'

'Of course,' she agreed in a businesslike way, but spoilt the effect completely by tripping over a root and landing on her bottom virtually in his lap.

'Tattie—' His arms closed around her and she thought he was smothering some laughter. 'Are you OK?'

'I'm fine! I'm…fine.' But she was not. She was far too conscious of his arms around her. She had not the slightest inclination to leave them—and she wasn't at all sure, she realised abruptly, that she liked being given such an easy way out from their marriage.

'Tattie?' He tilted her chin so he could look into her eyes.

An almost overwhelming longing came to her to run her fingers through his hair and offer him her mouth. In fact she could picture herself going a whole lot further, such as removing her clothes and having him tell her how lovely she was in an entirely *personal* way, rather than the impersonal way he had done so earlier.

She swallowed visibly and got extremely flustered just in case this husband she was about to part with could read her thoughts.

But he stilled her restless movements with a faint smile and her heart started to beat heavily, because she thought, she really thought, he was going to kiss her. He was certainly taking his time about something. He was certainly not attempting to put any distance between them, so she was resting against him and getting all hot and bothered again at the feel of him...

Then he said lightly, 'I'll go first.'

Her lips parted and her breath came raggedly, but all he did was ease himself away and stand up. Then he helped her up and—as if it was not adding insult to injury, did he but know it, she thought darkly—he dusted her bottom off.

'There. OK? Shall we head home?' He raised an eyebrow at her.

'Oh, definitely!'

There was a plop as a fish broke the surface of the billabong; there were ibis wading in the shallows, and an exquisite little kingfisher with turquoise wings sitting motionless in a bush. There were lush pink water lilies against the far bank. But all this faded from Tattie's consciousness because, despite her bright agreement, she could not stop staring into Alex's dark eyes.

And she had the terrible feeling that he *had* read her mind, that her awful confusion had given her away—if only she could tear her gaze away from his! It was not as if she could read what was in his eyes, but then, when had she ever been able to?

Perhaps this put some starch into her, because she finally found the will-power to turn towards the horses, and, after loading up, they rode home.

Two days later she found herself in Alex's arms once more, and once again in the most innocent way. She'd taken him to a rocky outcrop from where you could see forever over the station. They'd climbed to the top, and she'd pointed out all the landmarks to him: the gorge at the head of a tributary that wound its way into a mighty river; the mesa, or tabletop mountain, at the base of which her great-great-grandfather had camped when he'd taken up what would become known as Beaufort; the waterhole that had originally been the lifeblood of the station.

It was on the way down that he reached up and swung her down from the last rock—although she was perfectly capable of climbing down herself—and kept his hands on her waist.

She looked a question at him, but he merely studied her from head to toe—the sweat on her face and the tendrils of damp hair stuck to her cheeks, despite her hat, the outline of her mouth. The place where her slender neck disappeared into the V of her checked shirt and the soft hollows at the base of her throat. The swell of her breasts beneath her shirt.

'I could have done that,' she said huskily—anything to break the tension that was building up inside her.

'I know.' He smiled slightly. 'It just seemed the gallant thing to do.'

'Gallant!' something cried within her. If only he knew what a trial his being gallant was to her.

'Thanks,' she mumbled. 'Let me know when I can be gallant back.'

He laughed this time. 'We have a slight weight-ratio problem in that line, Tattie.'

'I don't doubt it.' She looked up at him and tried to block his tall proximity from her senses. 'In that respect you probably need a wife a little taller than five feet two...' She stopped and blinked rapidly, appalled at even mentioning the subject.

'Oh, I don't know. They say small packages can be very...sweet.' He looked her up and down again—comprehensively and, she thought, significantly, as if he was assessing her sweetest points, in fact.

'Oh. Well.' Aware that she was babbling, but unable to help herself, she ploughed on, 'I'm sure there are other ways of being gallant than swinging people off rocks.'

He moved his hands on her waist. 'Possibly. I'll let you know when I think you're being particularly gallant, Tattie.' But his eyes were *particularly* dark and wicked.

And he let her go and brought her horse to her.

Tattie managed to mount without any mishaps, considering the hammering of her pulses and the confused state of her mind. But all the way home she was asking herself a question—what was going on?

There was a surprise waiting for them at the homestead.

Marie and the farrier's wife had had a spring clean and Marie was engaged in cooking dinner.

'This is very nice of you, Marie,' Tattie said, 'but you didn't have to.'

'No problem,' Marie replied airily. 'I know how nicely you and Mr Constantin do things in Darwin—I saw a spread of your apartment in a magazine. And your mother used to do the same here when they had important visitors, so I thought...it would be nice, that's all. I got the good silver out and polished it up.'

Tattie hesitated, then went into the dining room to take a look.

The old oak table was set for two with the best china, shining silver, gleaming crystal and candles.

She came back to the kitchen. 'It looks lovely, Marie, but—'

'You've got plenty of time to have a soak in the tub and get changed,' Marie said. 'I won't be ready to dish up for another hour.'

Tattie eyed her as she moved busily from the stove to the counter, and knew she would disappoint her dreadfully if she didn't at least change—something her mother had always encouraged for dinner.

But she took the thought with her to the bathtub that Alex was responsible for this, she just knew it—what she didn't know was why.

She hadn't brought a lot of gear with her, but she had a pair of ivory stretch cotton trousers, a ruby silk-knit cowl-neck top and a pair of little-heeled patent ruby shoes.

Would have to do, she thought as she surveyed herself in her bedroom mirror and swung her newly washed hair. Then she rummaged through her dressing-table drawers and came up with a pair of flower earrings, roses edged in gold—she hadn't worn them since she was about sixteen but the main colour matched her top. She put them on, tucked her hair behind her ears and nodded at her reflection—Marie would appreciate the touch, she thought.

They met in the lounge and she wasn't surprised to see Alex had changed into a blue and white striped shirt with navy trousers.

'So this was your idea,' she said as she accepted a glass of sherry from him.

His eyebrows rose. 'Not at all. I merely got told you would be dressing for dinner. I gathered I'd better do likewise.'

She frowned. 'I still feel I'm being conspired against.'

'What's that supposed to mean?'

'Nothing,' she said hastily, and sipped her sherry. 'Well, it was you who probably got Marie all hepped up.'

'Why would I have that effect on her?'

She was sorely tempted to tell him he had that effect on all women but desisted—even in irony it wasn't an admission she cared to make at the moment.

'Whoever's idea, perhaps it wasn't such a bad one,' he said tranquilly while she battled with her demons. 'You look very nice, Tattie.' His gaze lingered on the ruby top and the flower earrings. 'One thing I can never take exception to is your dress sense.'

'What *do* you take exception to?' She regarded him, a true Beaufort beneath all her Beaufort ancestors.

He looked her over again. 'Not a lot. Shall we dine?'

It might have been roast beef—and you could get fairly sick of beef on a cattle station—but Marie had excelled herself. It was tender, faintly pink, melt-in-the-mouth beef, accompanied by Yorkshire pudding and all the trimmings. There was a brandy pudding to follow. And it was only after she'd served the pudding that Marie left them alone and retired to the head stockman's cottage.

'I feel exhausted,' Tattie said as she heard the back

door close at last. 'As if I've been under a searchlight, expected to come up to all Marie's *House & Garden* expectations or be instrumental in her living the Constantin lifestyle vicariously.'

Alex grinned and looked around. 'We have nowhere near the history the Beauforts have, so don't blame the Constantins, Tattie.'

'I feel like blaming them.' She pushed her dessert plate away and rose to pour the coffee. 'Shall we have this in front of the fire?'

He agreed, and when they were settled Tattie said thoughtfully, 'Alex, I don't know a great deal about you, your father's right.'

'I hope you're not going to harp on Flora Simpson; there is truly no more to be said. In more ways than one, now.'

Tattie rested her cheek on the plum velvet of her favourite wing chair and studied him. He was stretched out in an armchair on the other side of the fireplace, watching the fire, and he hadn't turned his head to her as he spoke. There had been a dry, unimpressed note in his voice too.

'No,' she said slowly, 'I'm not going to harp on Flora Simpson. You're right, there's no point. It's just that when I see you being the quintessential cattleman and grazier I can't help wondering how it fits in with your pearling background.'

Alex looked at her at last. 'When I was about seventeen my father decided to diversify and he threw me in at the deep end. He bought Mount Cookson, in the Territory, and told me it was mine to sink or swim with.'

'Of course you swam with it,' Tattie supplied with a tinge of bitterness in her voice.

He looked amused. 'I very nearly sank it. It was only buffalo that saved me.'

She looked interested. 'Go on. I know there's a bit of a market for buffalo meat, but not that much, I would have thought.'

'Strangely enough there's now a market for buffalo from whence they came—Indonesia and south-east Asia. I started exporting them, but as breeding stock. I still export buffalo from Cookson, as a matter of fact, although I've got back into cattle there as well.'

'The boy wonder.'

'Not really; there was a lot of hard work involved. And it helps to be able to turn your hand to a few things. For instance, I was always interested in mechanics, even as a kid.'

'So motors hold no mysteries for you, you only have to look a horse in the eye for it to know who's boss, you're a lot stronger than I am—all this is very depressing, Alex.'

He reached for his coffee. 'I've seen women who can strip a motor, prime a pump, stand no nonsense from a horse and throw a calf.'

'Big, tough women?' she hazarded.

He grinned at her. 'Generally, but not always. And you do ride beautifully, Tattie.'

'Thanks,' she murmured humbly. 'Alex, why do I get the feeling this week is designed to…give me a crash course in how *unsuitable* I am for the task I've set myself?'

He raised his eyebrows. 'I'm sorry if that's how it's turned out. I was only trying to help.'

'But you don't think I can do it?'

He grimaced.

'You can be honest, Alex.'

He sat forward with his cup in his hands. 'Tattie, no, I don't think you can do it.'

'And you're hoping, now that I've more or less seen it for myself, I'll pass the reins over to you and stay married to you?'

Alex put his cup down and stood up. He wandered to the fireplace, put another log on, then stood staring down at it with his hands shoved into his pockets. 'I take it that goes against the grain, Tattie?'

She shrugged. 'I don't have much option.'

'Then I have a suggestion.' He told her what it was.

# CHAPTER SIX

SHE stared at him with her mouth open for a long moment, then sat up suddenly. 'Say all that again!'

'The market for tourism is huge in this part of Australia.' He repeated himself patiently. 'Visitors flock from all over the world to see the Kimberley region and the Northern Territory. And many cattle stations are going into tourism as a sideline. They're offering accommodation—they're offering the cattle-station ''experience'' as well as the ''top end of Australia'' experience. The fantastic scenery, the Aboriginal culture, the fishing, the crocodiles—and I think Beaufort, and you, would be ideal for such a venture.'

'Why me?'

He looked around and shrugged. 'You're a Beaufort down to your socks, and you have your pioneering ancestors on the walls to prove it. People love that kind of history and authenticity. You have a lot of taste and discrimination when it comes to providing accommodation.' He gestured. 'This house is almost ready to go as it is—'

'That's my mother's taste and discrimination,' she said rapidly. 'But go on.'

'And you have a real feel for the country, Tattie. Few guests, even if they were paying through the nose for the experience, would fail to be moved by how much you love this place.'

She blinked several times. 'They needn't all pay

through the nose. We could have some bunkhouse guests.'

He smiled. 'Of course, you'd have to assess how you would feel about a lot of people visiting Beaufort.'

She looked around at her ancestors. 'If it would mean I could save Carnarvon, I wouldn't feel as if I'd let them down,' she said intensely. Her shoulders slumped and she swallowed. 'But it could take years to get going. I'd have to get a loan—'

'Or take me on as a partner.'

The words hung in the air.

She gazed at him warily.

He shrugged. 'It makes good business sense, Tattie. We already operate cruises between Broome and Wyndham; we have an advertising campaign well in place all over the world. We have access to a lot of people already coming here. We could give Beaufort a lot of promotion.'

'It's just...' she began.

'And you could pay me back every cent I put into this operation, as well as anything I spend on Carnarvon to get it out of the red.'

'What—' she licked her lips '—what about our marriage?'

'It stays as is.'

'Why?' she whispered. 'I thought you were ready to wash your hands of me.'

'I've changed my mind,' he said simply. 'Perhaps I've come to a better understanding of you, Tattie. Perhaps I'm still curious to know the *very good reason* you had for not wanting to change our marriage. Who knows?'

'I...I...' She closed her mouth frustratedly, then, 'How do you mean, a better understanding of me?'

He paused. 'You've got much more spirit than I gave

you credit for when I married you. And I don't know why but I've got the feeling you would love to prove yourself to me.' He put his head on one side and watched her narrowly.

She gasped. 'How did you know?'

But he only looked at her enigmatically.

'What if I don't want to stay married to you once I haven't got a cash-flow problem and Carnarvon is running well again?'

'We can reassess the situation then.'

Tattie discovered several emotions running through her. A sense of mystification, a sense of excitement, but also a little thread of relief. You're still hoping, aren't you? she asked herself. That he'll fall in love with you...

She looked away and trembled inwardly. It would seem she just couldn't help herself, but she hadn't been helped by these last few days. Days when she'd wondered if it mightn't be happening for him?

But there was nothing to indicate that now, she thought as she switched her gaze back to her husband, standing so tall and thoughtful beside the fire. No way to know, for her anyway, what was going through his mind.

'All right,' she said at last. 'I'll do it. Thank you.'

'I think this calls for a celebration.' He looked down at her. 'Shall we crack a bottle of champagne? To seal our—business—partnership?'

'Why not?' She went to get up.

'Stay there. I'll do it.'

She was seated exactly as he'd left her when he came back with the champagne and two glasses.

He popped the cork, handed her a foaming glass and pulled up the footstool. 'Cheers.' He sat down in front of her.

'Cheers.'

'I thought you'd be more excited. You were earlier.'

She tried to smile. 'I feel quite…stunned.'

'Drink up,' he suggested.

She drank half a glass, then he took it from her and stood up to pull her to her feet and into his arms.

'Alex?' she breathed.

'We may be business partners now, but we're also married, Mrs Constantin.'

'I thought you said we'd continue as is?'

His lips quirked. 'This is not something we've never done before, Tattie.' And he bent his head to tease her lips apart at the same time as he moved his hands down her back, sculpting her figure beneath the ruby silk jersey of her top and the thin cotton of her trousers.

He tasted of champagne—fresh and slightly tart—so did she, she guessed—and he felt hard but warm against her. Then he slipped his hands beneath her top, unerringly unclipped her bra and cupped her breasts.

She shuddered against him and slid her hands up to his shoulders, every inch of her body alive and urgently in need of his hands on it. Then she was kissing him and moving against him with a fire of desire surging through her.

And he led her to even more pleasure as he plucked her nipples and caressed her hips, all the time kissing her and allowing her the freedom of his body. To touch and stroke and marvel in his strength against her own small softness.

But just as her breathing reached a ragged crescendo and she was about to beg him to take her he brought their embrace down from the clouds and to a conclusion whereby there was a foot of space between them and no contact other than his hand on her elbow to steady her.

'What…?' she whispered uncomprehendingly.

'I don't think we should do anything—you might regret, Tattie,' he said.

'You… I…' She stopped and wildly sought for some understanding. But all she could see in his eyes was irony, and then she understood.

She took a deep breath. 'You're right. Goodnight, Alex.'

For a long time before she fell asleep her emotions defied description. What kind of a fool had she made of herself? How could she have let herself go like that? What game was he playing with her? Well, she thought she knew that. He was trying to show her she had no self-control when he really set his mind to arousing her, and forcing her to face the irony of it in the light of her refusal to consummate their marriage.

Which led her directly to an old question she'd asked herself at least once before…

Did she love or did she hate Alex Constantin?

By morning, when she woke in a mess of twisted bedclothes, all her questions seemed to be academic compared to the problem of how to face him again.

But when she forced herself to get dressed and appear at breakfast he had a surprise waiting for her—a puppy, the most adorable blue heeler with black-tipped ears and tail, and he simply put it in her arms.

'Oh! Where…? How…?' She gazed at him incredulously.

'One of the ringers' dogs had this litter six weeks ago and Jim just happened to mention it to me yesterday. So I went to have a look and picked him out myself. I hope he brings you a lot of joy and companionship.'

Tattie felt the warm little body squirm against her, got her nose licked, and was subjected to the anxious gaze of a baby removed from its mother and its siblings and not at all sure what on earth was going on.

'Oh... Oh, sweetheart,' she crooned, and hugged it. 'You're gorgeous!'

The puppy wriggled ecstatically, then closed its eyes and fell asleep.

Tattie raised a blue gaze full of wry amusement to Alex, and just about everything she'd planned to say to him flew out of the window. *What kind of game do you think you're playing with me, Alex Constantin? I no more want to be involved in a business partnership, let alone a marriage, with you than I want to fly to the moon. I not only don't like you, I don't approve of you...*

None of it got said, and then he took her further by surprise.

'Your mother and Doug Partridge are flying in today, to spend a few days with us, Tattie.'

'I... You've met him? The man she's planning to marry?' Tattie said, again incredulously.

'I have,' he agreed. 'I liked him. And I thought you'd enjoy having your mother help you with plans for the new project.'

'I would. That is to say...' She trailed off and gazed at him helplessly. Then, 'My mother hasn't, been well—' she swallowed '—meddling?'

He raised his eyebrows. 'Not as far as I know. Why?'

'Uh...it doesn't matter. What was I saying?'

'I got the impression you might have been trying to tell me you've changed your mind after last night?' He looked at her alertly.

Tattie closed her eyes, then looked down at the puppy in her arms. What did you do with a man who kissed

you witless, left you almost crazy with desire then got
you a puppy?'

'No,' she said at last, 'I guess not.'

'Wise thinking, Tattie. Shall we have breakfast?'

The next few days were quite hectic.

Natalie arrived with Doug Partridge and Tattie took
an immediate liking to him. A gentle giant of a man,
with a shock of grey hair, he loved painting the outback
and therefore was very happy to be at Beaufort. But what
really caused Tattie to widen her eyes was the way her
mother was suddenly seeing the countryside.

In fact, her mother was like a new person, and thrilled
with Alex's idea.

'You don't think Dad would have minded?' Tattie
asked her with a frown during their first discussion of it
all.

Natalie sat back. 'As I see it, darling, this is your best
option if you really want to do things on your own. I
mean, since you've explained the position with
Carnarvon, I could, in fact, help you out. Your father
left me the cash and you the properties, so—'

'No,' Tattie said definitely. 'I do want to do it on my
own and I certainly don't want to risk your assets in the
process.'

'I take it you don't want Alex to come to the party
either?' her mother enquired delicately.

'Well, he is, in a way. We've reached an agreement.
We'll stay married for the time being,' Tattie said without a tremor in her voice, which was not a true indication
of her feelings on the subject, 'but this will be a purely
business partnership between us.'

'I see.' Natalie gazed at her daughter and decided to
hold her peace. 'All right. Then let me tell you, Tatiana,

that I think this is a far better way for you to express
your love and the affinity you have with this place than
tearing yourself to pieces trying to be a cattleman. And
your father would have done anything he had to do to
hold on to Beaufort *and* Carnarvon. So rest easy, my
sweet. And go for it.'

One day I'll understand all this, Tattie thought the next
day.

They were all seated around the oak dining-room table
and ideas for enticing tourists to Beaufort were flying
thick and fast. Her mother was using her artistic skills
in sketches as she incorporated her and Tattie's ideas for
guest bedrooms. Alex and Doug were discussing ideas
for a bunkhouse where hardier tourists intent on getting
the ultimate cattle-station experience could be housed.

They'd all discussed the vehicles that would be required to show people the wonders of Beaufort, and the
horses needed for the hardier. And Alex had briefly run
through the more mundane matters, as he put it, pertain-
ing to running a tourist operation—the public-liability
policy they'd have to take out, the standards they'd have
to aspire to get a five-star rating and the hiring of per-
sonnel, since Tattie wouldn't be able to do it all on her
own.

But the mystery that Tattie was contemplating through
it all was the easy camaraderie that now existed between
her mother and her husband. At least, that was one mystery. Her present feelings for her husband were the most
mysterious of all. And just as she was about to shake
her head in a certain amount of disgust, because she truly
did not know where she stood with him and it was kill-
ing her, he turned to her.

'This is all very well,' he said with a lurking smile,

'the nuts and bolts. But it's going to be you who gets it off the ground, Tattie. Your touch with people, your feel for the place.'

The puppy, now named Oscar, since Tattie had discovered its mother's name was Lucinda, stirred in her lap and yawned prodigiously.

'Hear, hear!' Natalie said, and clapped her hands, and Doug smiled warmly at her.

Oscar sat up and barked his first bark, then looked surprised, as if he couldn't believe the sound had come from him.

They all dissolved into laughter. 'Thanks,' Tattie said, mysteriously feeling a lot better suddenly.


That night she got up around midnight, as she heard Oscar whimpering, and rushed into the lounge before he woke the whole house.

She'd fixed up a basket for him beside the fireplace, she'd put an old clock in with him, and even a hot-water bottle wrapped in a blanket, but he was sitting up looking piteously unhappy. Then he saw her and placed his paws on the rim of the basket. He experimented with his bark again in joyful recognition of her.

'Shush… Now, look here,' she whispered, kneeling down beside him, 'you've got to learn to sleep on your own. I know it's hard, after having a mum and six brothers and sisters with you, but don't forget you're going to grow up into the best, the bravest dog of them all!'

Oscar wagged his whole body, barked again, and took a flying leap into her lap.

'Oh, dear.' She stroked him. 'What am I going to do with you? I know what you're aiming for, young man! You want to come into my bed, but—'

'Once you start that, Tattie, you'll never get him out.'

They both turned to see Alex standing behind them. Oscar eyed him alertly, then experimented with another sound, a growl this time.

'Oh, the cheek of you!' Tattie marvelled, and hugged him.

'I can see that this might not have been such a great idea,' Alex said wryly.

It flew through Tattie's mind to say that, since no one else shared her bed, most notably not him, why shouldn't she allow her puppy the freedom of it while he was only such a baby?

But she put Oscar on the floor, then picked him up immediately and raced outside with him.

'Whoa! That was a close call!' She came back moments later, shivering from the cold night air with her nose pink and her hair flying.

'OK…' She put Oscar into Alex's arms and said to the puppy, 'Since this bloke gave you to me, I think you need to treat him with a bit more respect. In fact it's all right to make friends with him.'

'Thank you, Tattie,' Alex said ruefully, then addressed himself to the dog. 'Got that, mutt?'

Oscar hesitated, then licked Alex profusely.

'For heaven's sake, have him back.' He handed the dog over. 'I'm not keen on all that much friendship.'

'Don't worry, I know how to train a dog,' Tattie said. 'You see, he'll be a model—when he's a little older. Won't you, sweetness?'

Alex eyed his wife and her puppy and looked sceptical. But he said only, 'I hope you have a lot of fun with him.'

It was then that Tattie realised Alex was still dressed. 'Haven't you been to bed yet? It's past midnight!'

He looked down at his jeans and navy sweater. 'I was

just about to go to bed when I heard the dog. There were a few loose ends I wanted to tie up before I go tomorrow.'

'You're going tomorrow? I…I mean, I didn't know that,' she stammered, trying to cover up the surprise, and something else she might have exhibited.

'I was hoping to have a few more days, but something's come up. Your mother and Doug will be here for a while, though.' He looked down at her with a faint frown.

'Of course! I'll be fine, even when they're gone.' But would she? she wondered.

'And I'll be back as soon as I can. You're quite safe here now, Tattie. There are at least five men on Beaufort to protect you in the unlikely event of anyone coming somewhere this remote anyway.'

'Oh, that,' she said a little blankly. 'Do they know about someone trying to kidnap me?'

He paused, as if assessing her unpreparedness for the subject. 'Jim does. All that the others will know is that while you're here they should keep an eye out for you.'

Tattie grimaced.

'That makes good sense in any circumstances,' he said quietly.

'What's happened to Amy Goodall's friend?'

'He's been remanded without bail and will face at least two charges—carrying an unlicenced weapon and attempted kidnapping. You don't have to worry about him. But I have another suggestion to make, purely from a company point of view—company for you, I mean.'

'What's that?'

'Jim and Marie's eighteen-year-old daughter has finished school and may be forced to go to Perth or Darwin to get a job. They think she's too young, but the problem is how to keep her here. I suggested she move into the housekeeper's quarters here in the homestead in the role of trainee housekeeper…'

'Polly?' Tattie stared at him, then started to laugh. 'You know her?'

'Of course I know her! I grew up with her—and if ever there was a tomboy who could run a cattle station, she is it!'

'She seemed quite keen on the idea,' Alex said slowly. 'So's her mother.'

'I'm not surprised. Marie's been trying to tame Polly ever since I can remember.' Tattie was still chuckling.

'Perhaps Marie thinks you might succeed where she failed?'

Tattie sobered.

'She reckons that in her heart of hearts Polly would love to be everything you are,' Alex continued.

Tattie blinked. 'I didn't know that!'

He smiled enigmatically. 'Will you give it a try? If you succeed we could put her on the staff.'

'Well, yes. I think Polly loves Beaufort as much as I do, and Jim and Marie have always been wonderful to me. Of course! Just don't blame me if I don't succeed in turning her into a housekeeper.' Tattie hesitated and frowned. 'Alex, you take very good care of me, for a wife you…don't really want.'

There, it was out, she thought, although she closed her eyes and shivered inwardly at her temerity. But she just couldn't allow this unspoken war between them not to have some mention in dispatches before he flew away.

'Tattie?'

Her lashes flew up but he said no more for a long moment while he took in everything about her. Her white flannel pyjamas with their delicate pin-tucking and lace-trimmed collar, her bare feet, her hair, disarrayed but still gorgeous, her shadowed and confused cornflower-blue eyes.

And it occurred to Alex Constantin that his plan was working. She might tell him she didn't want to stay married to him for some mysterious 'very good reason', but one day she would go to bed with him because she couldn't help herself. A day of his choosing, however. And then this arranged marriage would become real whether she liked it or not...

So why, he wondered, did he not feel too good about himself?

'Tattie,' he said again, 'whatever is between us, you *are* my wife. You're also a nice person and my business partner. And your little dog is fast asleep, so now might be a good time to return him to his basket and get some sleep yourself.'

But what he got in return surprised him somewhat. A most rebellious spark entered those cornflower eyes and she drew herself up almost as if she'd love to fling his words right back at him, but at the last moment she turned the rebellion off and smiled sweetly at him.

'If you want to play games with me, Alex,' she said, also sweetly, 'be my guest. Just don't count on getting the opportunity to kiss me and walk away from me again, because I'll make damn sure it doesn't come up. Furthermore, until this dog learns to sleep through the night, he will sleep with me.' She turned on her heel and walked away.

His lips twitched as he watched her go, but for a moment he was almost unbearably tempted to replace Oscar in her arms and her bed—with himself. Well, well, he mused with a mixture of amusement and self-directed irony, that round goes to you, Tatiana Beaufort.

\*　　\*　　\*

Two months later, Polly dropped a plate, swore, then clapped a hand to her mouth and looked guiltily at Tattie.

'Thought I'd cured myself of that,' she said apologetically, 'dropping things and swearing, but I'm scared stiff, Tattie. There's eight people out there all waiting for me to make a fool of myself!'

'Polly.' Tattie put her hands on her shoulders. 'No one is waiting for you to make a fool of yourself. You can do this. You look terrific, and just think how proud your mum and dad are of you, not to mention me. And Alex, of course!' An afterthought that would surely do the trick, Tattie thought a little darkly.

Polly looked down at herself in her neat tunic top and long skirt, both professionally made. Then she touched her hair, which Tattie had rescued from blonde straw, bleached and dried by the sun, and persuaded her to get cut into a short bob. And she touched her face, which Tattie had shown her how to make up discreetly—and she took a deep breath.

'I guess I can, thanks to you, Tattie.'

'OK. Now I'm going to join the guests, but if you need me just tell me quietly.'

Polly nodded, and after a last look around Tattie took a deep breath and went through to the dining room, where dinner was almost due to be served.

It was their maiden voyage, in a manner of speaking. Their first group of guests and a most discerning group at that—at least Tattie assumed so, because they'd just come from a Constantin cruise, which would have set them back a small fortune. They were a group of Americans travelling together and they'd arrived two hours ago.

In that time, and earlier, things had not gone smoothly. Marie, who was supposed to be in charge in the kitchen, had developed a bout of hay fever that had to be seen to be believed and had been sent to bed, the only thing she was good for. Natalie was supposed to have flown in earlier in the day but had sprained her ankle. Alex had been asked to stay away and had—when she could really do with him, Tattie thought irrationally—and Oscar had pulled a sheet off the washing line and chewed it up on the front lawn so that it resembled confetti.

Thus it was that only she and Polly were on hand. All the same, the dining table looked wonderful beneath a full complement of the Beaufort silver, crystal and fine porcelain, the guests were happy with their rooms, and it was now up to her to provide them with a wonderful experience.

Three hours later, she and Polly sat in the kitchen drinking champagne with their shoes kicked off, the door firmly closed and Oscar asleep in his basket.

'What a night!' Polly said enthusiastically. 'But we did it! You know the oldest guy, the one who looks to be in his eighties? He actually pinched me on the bottom and nearly got his dessert poured all over him!'

Tattie giggled like a girl. 'I saw your face and held my breath. Oh, wow! You're right, what a night, but they loved it and you were wonderful.'

'They loved *you*. OK.' Polly looked around at the colourful chaos of the kitchen and groaned.

'I'll help.' Tattie drained her glass. 'At least tomorrow night's a barbecue and your mum might be better.'

'We've got to get through tomorrow's day before we get to tomorrow night,' Polly said ruefully, then looked at Tattie curiously. 'I just wish Alex had been here to see you tonight, Tattie. You looked so…regal.'

Tattie grimaced. 'I asked him to stay away. Sometimes he makes me feel self-conscious.'

Polly smacked her palm on her forehead. 'Know exactly what you mean. Dad has the same effect on me.'

It was midnight before Tattie got to bed, but at least she was secure in the knowledge that everything was as it should be and ready for the day's activities. But Polly's remark about Alex had stayed with her, although her reply had been true to an extent. It was the way things were between her and Alex that would have made her self-conscious did Polly but know it.

Of course, Polly was as crazy about Alex as every other woman he came in contact with, so she had no reason to suspect he could be quite…really *quite* diabolical at times, Tattie thought as she lay down with a sigh and switched her bedside light off.

Such as implementing a truce between them that was a terrible farce. But what option did she have but to go along with her husband, when he came and went from Beaufort, at his charming best in front of her mother, her staff and the whole world whilst keeping an absolutely scrupulous distance from her in private? None, she answered herself. And she'd done it for a whole year so why couldn't she do it now?

'I don't know,' she whispered into the darkness. 'It just tears me apart these days to have nothing resolved, to suspect that he'll wear me down so I'll agree to stay married to him, really married. On top of all that I was the one who threw down the gauntlet,' she reminded herself gloomily. 'Come to that, I was the one who started this whole cat and mouse game in the first place.'

She sniffed, and Oscar, who had been transported fast asleep in his basket to her bedroom, woke up and leapt onto the bed.

'Oh, no,' she murmured. 'We've got an agreement, now, remember? You can sleep in here on the condition you stay in your basket, young man! As a matter of fact, I'm not game to let you sleep anywhere else in case you chew things—which reminds me, I'm still very cross with you! It took us hours to clear up that sheet.'

But Oscar ignored her, possibly because the tone of her voice was not consistent with her words, and he snuggled down beside her.

Tattie sighed. And put her arm round him. 'Just this once, then.'

But at least she fell asleep shortly afterwards.

Two days later she and Polly farewelled their first guests and were on the receiving end of the most ravishing compliments.

Things had gone much more smoothly on day two. Marie had woken clear of her hay fever and able to take over the kitchen. Polly and Tattie had escorted the party on a tour of the property, some on horseback, others in a four-wheel-drive vehicle, and nothing had gone wrong. No horse had bolted or put its foot in a hole—and Beaufort had done the rest.

The barbecue under the stars last night around a big bonfire had been a huge success. They'd sung songs and Polly had electrified them all with her whip-cracking expertise. And now they were going, all swearing they'd be back, and not only that—they'd also tell all their friends about the best 'top end' experience they'd had.

And, possibly because she'd been so inundated, Tattie hadn't heard Alex fly in, so it took her completely by surprise to turn from waving the bus off and almost bump into him.

'Oh! I didn't hear you arrive!'

'So I gathered. Would I be right in assuming you've had an outstanding success?'

'Would you ever!' Polly glowed. 'I've had four invitations to go to America!'


'I take it you've tamed Polly?'

Tattie and Alex were having lunch on the veranda, alone for once, when he made his remark.

Tattie shook her head. 'Not really. Smoothed a few corners, that's all. They just adored her as herself—a dinkum Aussie girl. Alex, if this is a real success, Polly will have to take a lot of the credit.'

'Tell me about it all?'

She did so, making him laugh with the disasters of the first day then the highlights of the rest of it.

But he sobered as she ran out of anecdotes and studied her. 'You're exhausted.'

She couldn't disagree, although she said, 'It's got to get easier.'

'Have you got any bookings this week?'

'No, but next weekend is a big one—a full house and a party of six in the bunkhouse.'

'Come to Darwin with me for a few days.'

Her eyes widened. 'Why?'

'You need a break.'

'I... Not really; I'll be fine, and there's so much to do!'

'Anything Polly, Marie and your mother and the rest of the staff can't handle?'

'Uh...Mum's sprained her ankle.'

'It's better. She rang me this morning to apologise for

having to desert you. She and Doug are happy to come for the next influx.'

Tattie looked at her plate of cold meat and salad, then sipped the glass of wine he'd insisted on pouring her. 'There's Oscar.'

At the sound of his name Oscar pricked up his ears and placed his front paws on Tattie's knee.

'Bring him,' Alex said.

'Oh, I don't... I mean, in an apartment—'

'You'll just have to take him for regular walks.'

Tattie stared at him wordlessly.

He held her gaze with his dark eyes unfathomable for a long moment. Then he said drily, 'My mother is having a hip replacement in two days. She's missing you and wants to see you before she goes in. I think she's really nervous about it all.'

Tattie bit her lip. 'Why didn't you say so in the beginning?'

He didn't answer, but his look said it all.

She had a chat with Oscar before she went to bed.

'Sweetheart,' she said seriously, 'I'm going away for a few days. I would love to take you with me but I think it would be really difficult—for both of us. So I'm going to leave you with Polly. Please be good for her, and I'll be back before you know it!'

Oscar gazed at her soulfully.

'I'll tell her to let you sleep on my bed,' Tattie promised, then grimaced. 'Well, maybe not, but rest assured, when I get back it'll be like old times because you and I are a team!'

Oscar crawled into her lap and licked her chin and she hugged him close.

But it was harder than even she had anticipated to leave him the next morning.

# CHAPTER SEVEN

AT MIDDAY the next day she was standing in the middle of the lounge of their Darwin apartment, looking around a little dazedly.

Alex put their bags down and went to open the shutters and sliding glass doors. It was a magnificent dry-season Darwin day, warm and clear with no smoke from bush fires, and two navy boats were steaming smartly towards Stokes Wharf.

'Doesn't feel like home any more?' he queried as he took in her expression.

She opened her mouth to say no, then changed her mind. 'It just feels a bit strange to be back.'

'Perhaps you *should* have brought Oscar,' he said drily.

Tattie grimaced. 'I tremble to think what Oscar could do to this place,' she said, 'if he was left to his own devices.'

But of course the other reason she'd left Oscar behind was for an excuse to get back to Beaufort as soon as possible.

'Is that an admission that you haven't been as successful a dog trainer as you thought?'

Tattie hesitated, belatedly realising that Alex was somewhat annoyed. She wondered why. 'He's only three and a half months old,' she said quietly. 'You... Are you cross with me about something? Other than Oscar?'

He faced her squarely, then shrugged and grinned reluctantly. 'I'm beginning to regret giving you that dog because it's obvious he means more to you than just about anything else. But that is actually rather a "dog in the manger" attitude on my part, so don't worry about it.'

Her lips parted incredulously. 'You...couldn't be jealous!'

He strolled across the carpet, took her chin in his hand and kissed her very lightly. 'For my sins, yes, I could.'

She was transfixed by the glint in his eyes, the feel of his fingers still on her chin, and the whole dangerously exciting experience of Alex Constantin in close proximity with that look in his eye. He wore a bush shirt and jeans, he flew his plane with consummate ease, as he did just about everything, and he was so much pure man her knees felt like buckling at the thought that he could be jealous over her.

But he released her almost immediately, shoved his hands in his pockets and changed the subject completely. 'Look, I'm sorry about this, but I've asked my parents over to dinner tonight. You know how my mother insists on personally supervising an eight-course banquet at home, and I don't think she's up to a restaurant. Could you manage that? The operation is tomorrow, so it will take her mind off it.'

Tattie came down to earth with a bump and swallowed. 'Uh...of course. I've got time to shop and...all the rest.'

'Good girl.' This time he kissed her on the top of her head, most impersonally, and added, 'I've got to go to work for the afternoon, so I'll be out of your hair.'

He turned to go, then turned back. 'By the way, I've got a surprise for you.'

All she could do was raise her eyebrows at him.

'Tonight, Tattie. See you.' And he was gone.

\* \* \*

It turned out to be a long, dithery afternoon for Tattie.

She shopped, then had to go out again for the things she'd forgotten. She prepared dinner, but several times had to stop herself from seasoning dishes twice.

I'm a nervous wreck, she told herself, or, to put it more accurately, I don't know if I'm on my head or my heels—and all because Alex is jealous of Oscar! Unless this is some new direction of the game?

Finally she got things under control and went to have a relaxing soak in the tub. Which turned out to be not so relaxing on account of her churning emotions, and *they* were responsible for her not hearing Alex come home. Thus it was that just as she stepped out of the bath the door opened and Alex stood there.

She froze on the step up to her raised, shell-shaped bath and he stopped abruptly in the doorway.

Then he murmured, 'My apologies, Tattie. Things were so quiet I wondered if you'd run off again, or if someone had kid…' He stopped.

'No. As you see.' She closed her eyes and could have died, because there was absolutely nothing of her that was not on offer for him to see.

'I do. You look like Venus rising out of her shell. I'll bring you a towel.' He plucked a jade towel from the rail and brought it over to her. 'Only much lovelier than Venus to my mind,' he said softly, coming to stand right in front of her.

Their gazes clashed, cornflower-blue and dark, almost black. Then his gaze slipped up and down her sleek, pearly body, from her high little breasts with their velvety tips right down to her toes.

Once again Tattie was transfixed. He handed her the towel and she took it, but the will to wrap it around her seemed to have deserted her. Nor could she tear her gaze from his.

'Tattie,' he said very quietly, deep in his throat and he once again flicked that dark gaze up and down her curves, then paused.

And he sniffed. He definitely sniffed, and half turned from her, and she was ready to die of mortification—until she caught it as well: the aroma of burning meat.

'Oh, no! My dinner,' she moaned. 'This is just the worst day of my life!' And she wound the towel round her swiftly and leapt down the step, straight into his arms.

He picked her up.

'Alex, no, I haven't got time for this,' she protested. 'I cannot offer your mother a burnt meal!'

'Let's see what we can do, then.' He carried her through to the kitchen, put her down and grabbed a cloth with which to open the smoking oven. When the smoke cleared her piece of roast pork revealed itself as burnt black.

Tattie looked at the temperature gauge unbelievingly. It was far too high, and she put her hand to her mouth in despair.

Alex looked alertly from her to the pork. 'OK. Let's stay calm,' he recommended. 'What else have you got?'

'I've got smoked salmon for the entrée and fruit salad and ice cream for dessert, but I cannot offer them only an entrée and a dessert,' she said tragically.

He tucked the corner of the towel more securely between her breasts. 'I have the solution. There's a take-away I know of that does fantastic spare-ribs. I'll ring them.'

'Your mother would die rather than eat take-away food!'

'That's a good thing,' he said. 'She won't have had any of their spare-ribs, so she won't know it's a take-away.'

'But—isn't it too late?'

He smiled into her deeply worried eyes. 'I've been a very good customer of theirs while you've been doing great deeds at Beaufort, Tattie. They'll rush it here with all the trimmings, and if you just point me in the direction of suitable serving dishes no one will know the difference.'

She breathed a sigh of relief, and the towel slipped a bit as she gestured towards a cupboard.

Once more he tucked the corner more securely between her breasts, but this time his fingers lingered on her skin.

'May I make another suggestion, Tattie?'

She stared a question up into his dark eyes with her breath starting to come raggedly again.

'That you take yourself off and leave all this to me.'

'Yes, all right,' she murmured, but her feet refused to move.

'What's more,' he said softly, but with a most wicked glint in his eye, 'it might be a good idea to wear your least sexy clothes tonight, otherwise I doubt if you and I will get through this evening, and we don't really want to shock my parents rigid, do we?'

His gaze lingered on her throat, the smooth, rounded skin of her shoulders, the valley where the towel was tucked between her breasts, the flare of her hips beneath the jade material.

Tattie swallowed and, although he wasn't touching her, she could feel the graze of his end-of-day stubble on her cheeks, the hard lines of his body on hers and, above all, she could remember all too well what pleasure he could inflict on her with his hands and mouth.

'Tattie?'

'I'm going,' she whispered, and fled for the sanctuary of her bedroom.


Her least sexy clothes!

She surveyed her wardrobe a little wildly and finally came up with a long navy linen dress. It had a Peter Pan collar of off-white Thai silk, cap sleeves and a row of mother-of-pearl buttons down the front. And it was straight, not fitted, although it did have a slit up one side—but a very discreet one. She slipped on a pair of plain navy blue shoes with little heels, then sat down in front of the dressing table to tackle her hair, her make-up, but most of all the still stunned look in her eyes. She couldn't go back out looking like that, she told herself as she brushed her hair and wielded the minimum amount of make-up—a light foundation, the faintest touch of blusher and some lip gloss.

Better—well, a bit, she decided as she studied herself critically, and for the first time in her life longed acutely for a drink. She stood up and sprayed her perfume on, and the door clicked open. It was Alex with a glass in his hands.

'Brought you a Scotch, ma'am, and the information that everything is under control. The ribs have arrived.'

He put the glass on the dressing table and looked her up and down with his lips quirking.

'Now, that dress,' he said gravely, 'makes you look like a nun. Which is a challenge in its own right for any red-blooded man. You've got about ten minutes, Tattie.' And he left, closing the door behind him.

Tattie sat down and murmured several very unladylike

epithets her convent school would have been horrified to hear issue from her lips. Then she took a strong swallow of her drink and closed her eyes. Should she change? How did you cope with Alex in this mood? How was she going to get through the evening, and most of all…what awaited her at the end of it?

Then she heard the doorbell chime. It had to be George and Irina. She took another sip of her drink, squared her shoulders and sighed deeply—and went to entertain her parents-in-law as well as cope with her husband.

In point of fact, Alex behaved beautifully.

And Irina, limping painfully and using a cane, was genuinely thrilled to see her. So was George.

'My dear Tatiana, I've missed you so much! I would have loved to come and see Beaufort and what you've done, but as you see I'm an old crock these days.' Irina enveloped Tattie in an emotional hug.

A sliver of guilt pierced Tattie for having run off the way she had—made worse by how nice they were being about it. Unless Alex had coached them…

But dinner progressed without a hitch, and Irina said of the spare-ribs, 'My dear, that was delicious—you excelled yourself!'

Tattie opened her mouth but intercepted a warning glance from Alex, which went along the lines of—*Don't you dare say a word!*

She shut her mouth and went to get the fruit salad and ice cream.

It was while she was pouring the coffee that Alex produced his surprise. He'd suggested they have their coffee in the den, where the television was, and he slipped a video into the machine.

Tattie went on pouring the coffee, then stopped as she, in her pink linen dress, appeared on the screen.

Irina clapped her hands. 'I can't see this often enough!'

'Tattie hasn't seen the edited version yet.' Alex took the coffee-pot from her and told her to sit down.

'My dear, you are excellent,' George pronounced. 'A wonderful advertisement for Constantin pearls.'

'Oh, dear, this is embarrassing,' Tattie murmured, but not long afterwards she lost herself in the video as it brought back memories of the lovely time she'd spent with Alex at the pearl farm and in the Drysdale River.

But her cheeks burned as they all, including Alex, congratulated her again as the video finished.

'You may have to watch this little girl, son,' George said jovially. 'Hollywood could steal her!'

Alex grinned and slipped another video into the machine. 'Now this one is the unedited version of the one we made for Beaufort.'

Tattie sat up. She'd forgotten about the two days they'd had a film crew on the station to make a promotional video. And she blinked as Oscar, with a shoe in his mouth, bounded onto the screen with her and Polly in hot pursuit. Polly could be heard swearing, then was seen clapping a hand over her mouth and saying, 'Sorry, Tattie, strike that!'

Tattie turned to Alex accusingly. 'You didn't!'

He nodded. 'I did. They had their cameras rolling almost all the time. Watch this.'

She looked back at the screen and there she was on horseback, describing the wonders of a billabong, until her horse got stung by a bee and reared up and took off with her.

'That was take one,' Alex said.

'I don't believe this,' Tattie said.

This time, looking quite windblown as she started her spiel, with Polly holding the horse just to be on the safe side, she said slowly and clearly on the video, 'There are more billabongs in this wonder... That's not right, is it?' And the prompter could be heard in the background correcting her... 'there are more wonders in this billabong...'

'That was take two,' Alex murmured, 'but you ain't seen nothing yet.'

In take three she'd only uttered two words when her horse decided to relieve itself at length.

And in take four Tattie had almost got through her speech on the wonders of billabongs when Polly started to do a demented jig at the same time as she was heard to say, 'There are also bloody green ants around billabongs and I'm standing on a nest. Ouch!' And the camera panned around to see that everyone was convulsed with laughter.

Tattie had to wipe her eyes in the civilised safety of Darwin as she remembered that hilarious day. 'I think it took seven takes to get it right,' she said, still laughing.

'Oh, look,' Irina said as the video finally rolled to a close, 'I haven't laughed so much for years. Thank you, Alex and Tattie. And thank you so much for coming home to be with me during this operation.'

Tattie took Irina's hand in hers. 'I can't wait to show you Beaufort in the flesh. As soon as you've got this little business out of the way you must come and stay. Both of you,' she said warmly to George.

'A successful evening.'

Tattie turned to see that Alex had come out onto the veranda after seeing his parents off.

'Thanks to you. She really is struggling, isn't she?'

'Mmm... We've been trying to persuade her to have this done for quite a while now, but you know how much she hates hospitals and is scared to death of operations. Hip replacements have a great rate of success, though.'

'Does she...? Do they...? They didn't ask any questions about me leaving Darwin. Did you warn them off, Alex?'

'Of course.'

'How?'

'I told them it was something you needed to get out of your system, that's all.' He shrugged.

Tattie went still. 'Is that what you genuinely believe?'

He glanced down at her and smiled fleetingly. 'Isn't it, Tattie?'

'It's much more than that!'

He shrugged. 'All the same, I'm at a slight disadvantage here, Tatiana. No one can quite understand why I haven't bedded you and got all this nonsense out of the way.'

She made a kittenish sound of pure outrage. 'It is not nonsense, Alex Constantin!'

'*I* wasn't saying it was nonsense. I was only faithfully reporting to you how others, your mother included, view it. And the slightly awkward position it puts me in, that's all.'

'She hasn't—my mother hasn't *dared* to express such an opinion,' Tattie got out, more in sincere hope than from conviction, because the circles of her mother's mind were not always predictable.

'Perhaps not on what I should do about it, but she was the one who told me you needed to get this out of your system—your obsession with saving Carnarvon like a true Beaufort,' he said drily.

Tattie spluttered something incomprehensible, then took aim at the only thing left in her sights. 'Leaving that aside, it must be a little galling to know that your reputation with women is suffering, Alex.'

But it bounced off him harmlessly.

'I can live with it, Tattie,' he drawled. 'For one thing, they're only our families. For another, they don't know the real story.'

Several sequences flashed through Tattie's brain. The number of occasions he had kissed her and found her not unwilling at all. The occasion he had been the one to call a halt when she had not had the will-power or the desire to do so. Desires quite in the opposite direction, you might say, she thought, and winced. And only this evening, when all that had saved her from giving herself to him had been a piece of burnt roast pork.

But in light of what he'd just told her, even if he claimed it didn't bother him what their families thought, *she* thought she could see a pattern in the game, and that pattern was not that he was falling in love with her or genuinely jealous of Oscar—perish the thought, she marvelled bitterly—but a determination to make this arranged marriage work.

'Alex, I'm going to bed and I'm going to lock my door, because you're still playing games with me,' she told him through her teeth.

He put his hand on her arm to detain her and his mouth was hard, the lines of his face grim. 'Don't bother to lock your door, Tattie. I wouldn't dream of trying to scale your ivory tower tonight. But let's get something straight. All this blew up out of nothing—yes, perhaps I wasn't so tactful but I was honest. Your blow-hot, blow-cold approach is not. If you want me as I want you, at least admit it. And if you don't, you must *really* be an incredible actress.' He released her arm and stepped back.

She gasped as if he'd struck her. Then she ran away from him, and she did lock herself into her bedroom.

She spent the next afternoon at the hospital, after Irina's operation.

She and Alex weren't talking—not in private anyway—and it helped to have something to do, although it wasn't a lot, as Irina slowly came round. But at least she could relieve George from time to time. Alex spent an hour with his mother when she regained consciousness and brought her a lovely spray of yellow cymbidium orchids in a pewter bud vase exquisitely studded with natural keshi pearls.

Tattie watched him during the hour he spent with his mother and found it hard to equate this man with the grim stranger of the night before. He made Irina laugh and he obviously made her feel cherished, so that you could see the terrors of hospitals and operations fading.

After an hour Irina told him to take George away and give him dinner. 'Tattie will stay with me until you bring him back, won't you, my dear?'

'Of course,' Tattie agreed.

'He's so kind to me, Alex is,' Irina murmured when they'd gone. 'In fact, he's a fine man, my son!'

'He is.' Tattie swallowed and wondered what was coming. But Irina fell asleep until George and Alex reappeared.

George whispered to her that he would take over now and Alex would take her home. 'You look really tired, but thank you for everything today and last night,' he added.

She got up and cast an uncertain glance at Alex; she couldn't help herself.

He said quietly, 'Come home, Tattie.'

'You look exhausted.'

They'd just got into the apartment and he put his keys on the hall table and pulled off his jacket and tie.

'Can you eat anything?'

'No… I don't know…' She couldn't go on.

He grimaced. 'Listen, I'm not about to resume hostilities. Go into the den, put your feet up and I'll bring you something. And thank you for being with my mother today.' He turned away.

She went into the den and did as she was told. Presently he arrived with a tray and put before her some toasted cheese sandwiches and a pot of fragrant Earl Grey tea, but he had nothing for himself.

'Don't you want some of this?' she queried.

'No. I ate with Dad.' He moved to an armchair and sprawled out in it. He waited until she'd eaten her sandwiches to say, 'By the way, I heard from Beaufort today. Your mother and Doug have arrived and all is well, although Oscar appears to be missing you. He hasn't chewed a single thing since you left.'

Tattie smiled and sipped her tea. 'Perhaps he's growing up. Either that or I'm a bad influence on him.' Her smiled faded and she looked suddenly desolate.

Alex sat up. 'He's missing you, Tattie, that's all. Look, let's just concentrate on getting my mother over this then you can go back to Beaufort and we'll—' he gestured rather wryly '—come to some arrangement. But it's stupid for us to carry on in a state of armed neutrality at the moment.'

'All right,' she said slowly, and finished her tea. 'But

would you mind if I went to bed now? I do seem to feel exhausted.'

'Of course not.' His eyes were alert as he scanned her pale, weary face, and he stood up and came over to her. 'Goodnight, my dear. Sleep well. It's not the end of the earth, you know.'

It may not be for you, Alex, she said in her mind as she leant back against her bedroom door, but I feel as if I've been run over by a steamroller. I don't know what to think. I don't even seem to know myself too well any more. Hasn't that always been the problem, though? What's between us may not be cataclysmic for you, but it is for me...

And, to make matters worse, Irina was transferred into Intensive Care the next morning with post-operative complications. There followed four awful days while her doctors battled to save her life.

'If you want to go back to Beaufort, your next lot of guests are due to arrive shortly,' Alex said to her at one point. 'I—'

'Do you really think I'd do that?' she interrupted.

He looked ten years older, with harsh lines scored beside his mouth, and he was grey from lack of sleep. 'It's not that, but—'

'Alex,' she said more gently, 'between my mother, Polly, Doug and Marie, they can cope. I'm not going anywhere. But I am going to lay down the law here. You must go home and get some sleep. I promise I'll call you if there's any change.'

'Dad—'

She interrupted again. 'I'll be there with him at her bedside.'

\*   \*   \*

Two days later they got the news that, although there was a long road back to full health in front of Irina, she was out of danger. And for the first time they were able to go home together.

It was a balmy evening, and while Tattie made them a meal Alex simply stood on the veranda, staring out over the harbour as the last of the daylight faded with a light show made unique by the dust and smoke from bush fires that were so much part of the Northern Territory at this time of the year.

Nor did he turn, although he must have heard her, and after she'd put the plates down she went to stand next to him at the railing.

He said, 'I was so afraid she was going to die without ever seeing the grandchildren she yearned for. I really felt I'd failed her.'

'Not you—me,' Tattie whispered.

He didn't look at her and shook his head. 'No. It's part of our culture and heritage, Tattie. You'd have to be Greek to understand it. I don't think mostly Anglo-Saxon with a dash of Russian can really give you the same...whatever it is.' He shrugged. 'And you certainly can't be held accountable for it.'

'But you've been a wonderful son to her, Alex. She adores you.'

'I still feel as if I've let her down. I still...' He moved his shoulders restlessly. 'She might have driven me mad at times with the way she tried to run my life but I still...would be devastated to lose her.'

'I know what you mean, and she isn't even my mother,' Tattie said softly. 'There's just something about Irina that you can't help loving. So much warmth, and she's so genuine—she's just one of those people who makes your life better for knowing her.'

He took a deep, shuddery breath and said huskily, 'Thank you for that.'

And something broke within Tattie, something that felt like a knot unravelling, releasing the certainty that, whatever happened in the future, she had never loved Alex Constantin more than she did right now. Was it because she'd never seen him so defenceless before? she wondered. Was it because she had seen real, painful emotion and a very human side to him over the last few days—perhaps for the first time?

She shook her head, unable to answer herself or fight the tide of longing that swamped her to at least bring him some comfort. And she slipped her arm around his waist and laid her head below his shoulder.

He tensed, but she ignored it and rubbed her cheek against his shirt.

'Tattie—no,' he said barely audibly. 'This is very sweet of you, but—'

'It's not sweet. I can't help it, that's all, and I'd appreciate it if you didn't make me feel like a teenager.'

She felt his chest jolt with sudden laughter. But he sobered immediately and there was evident strain in his voice as he said, 'What do you want me to do? Kiss you and walk away from you, Tattie?'

'No. I want you to leave it all to me, Alex, just this once. Come inside.' She took his hand.

'Dinner…' he started to say.

She looked at the meal she'd prepared going cold on the veranda table. 'Dinner can wait.'

Her bedroom was dark, so she switched on a bedside lamp.

Alex was standing in the middle of the room, looking

around at the lovely cream and hyacinth decor with a slightly wry expression.

Tattie went to him and put her hand in his. 'I know what you're thinking.'

He looked down at her with his eyebrows raised.

'That this is a little like storming the Bastille?' she suggested.

His lips twitched. 'I was beginning to doubt that I'd ever use this room for its rightful purpose.'

Tattie raised his hand to her mouth and kissed his knuckles. 'At this moment in time,' she said barely audibly, 'it seems very right to be in here, together.'

He touched her hair. 'At this moment in time, Tattie, there's nowhere else I'd rather be, but—'

'Let's just do it,' she whispered, and moved into his arms.

They closed about her, but she could sense he was still holding back, that he was still tense.

'Tattie, there's a point of no return in these matters.'

She raised her eyes to his and they were clear and unshadowed. 'I won't do that to you,' she promised.

He smiled, but there was still a question in his eyes.

'You're wondering if I...know much about it at all?'

'Perhaps.'

'No, I don't,' she conceded. 'In fact, I have no idea where to go from here, so I guess I must have a lot of faith in you, Alex, because I really would like to...go on from here, with you.'

He hesitated briefly and remembered that he had actually planned this, the only difference being that it was to have been a time of his choosing. Was it ironic that she had beaten him to the draw? Was it supremely ironic, he wondered, that he should be worried about taking unfair advantage of her when she herself had opened up the way for him?

Then she stood on her toes and kissed him softly. 'Is this…a good direction to take?' she breathed against the corner of his mouth.

He said her name on a tortured breath and pulled her so close she could barely breathe. 'It's excellent,' he murmured, and started to kiss her deeply.

And in the end he was the one who took control of their lovemaking; he couldn't help himself. As she clung to him dazedly she was more than happy to surrender the lead. 'Oh—I really don't know how to go on!' she said raggedly.

'Tattie,' he said on a breath, 'do you want to stop?'

'No!' She looked up at him, her eyes horrified. 'I didn't mean that. It's just that it might be an idea if I surrendered the lead to you, in a manner of speaking.'

Her arms were around his neck, his hands were on her hips, her shoes were kicked off, the buttons of the blouse she wore with a long georgette skirt were undone to her waist, and a wicked glint came into his eyes as he looked down at her.

'You were doing very well in the lead, Mrs Constantin, I don't think you have to worry about that.'

'All the same—is it too soon to go to bed?'

He laughed softly. 'No. Any more of this and I could become a basket case.'

Her eyes widened and her lips parted.

He kissed her and picked her up. 'Let me show you.' And he carried her to the bed.

But far from being a basket case, and despite his earlier exhaustion, Alex Constantin went out of his way to make love to her with the most exquisite finesse. He undressed her carefully and told her how lovely she was, until she couldn't help but believe him. And his fingers wrought a devastating trail of fire down her body at the same time.

'I'd like to do the same to you,' she whispered once.

'Be my guest,' he replied, and took his clothes off.

'Oh,' she said huskily when they were in each other's arms with nothing between them. 'I'm sure this isn't really red-hot sex but I don't think I could stand much more.'

He lifted his head; he'd been tugging her nipples gently between his teeth. 'This is as good as it gets, Tattie.'

'Really? For you too?' she gasped.

'Let me show you.' And he eased his weight onto her and all the unfamiliar sensations, instead of frightening her, became a matter of urgency, lovely, rapturous, extremely compelling, and obviously as compelling for him. She was lost for words at last, and she gave herself up completely to Alex's stewardship of her body, following all his leads as he led her to sheer heaven and held her hard in his arms while they both shuddered with the intensity of it.

'OK?' He brushed her hair off her face with his fingers.

She didn't answer because she still couldn't speak.

He grinned and kissed her, and she cuddled up to him with a sigh.

Then she found some words at last. 'I was supposed to be the one bringing you some comfort.'

'You did. I feel like a new man.'

'Really?' She raised her eyes to his a little wryly.

'Yes, really, Tattie. By the way, what did you think *really* red-hot sex meant?'

'Ah. I had visions of, well, doing it anywhere, for example. In cars, on carpets, in hay lofts—'

'I could always arrange that, although personally I'm happier with a bed.'

She ignored him, but with a severe little look. 'I had visions of exotic underwear and strange positions and golden, leopard-like women—'

'Strange positions can play havoc with one's back,' he offered gravely.

'Let me finish—to be honest, really red-hot sex frightened the life out of me.'

He laughed. 'I'm not surprised! But are you trying to say you associated me with all that?'

She went to say yes, then bit her lip. And she said instead, 'I guess you just don't know what you're in for until you do it.'

'No. So how was it?'

She closed her eyes and thought back for a moment, and felt herself go all goosefleshy. 'The most marvellous experience of my life,' she said simply.

He gathered her closer and murmured against the corner of her mouth, 'One day I'll remind you you said that, but thank you.'

Her lashes fluttered up. 'Shouldn't I have said it?'

'You have my permission to say it to me any time you like.'

'So...? Was it too ingenuous or something like that?' she queried, sounding suddenly awkward.

His dark gaze sharpened and she thought he was about to say something. Then he changed his mind. 'No. I'll always remember it.'

Not much later she fell asleep in his arms.

# CHAPTER EIGHT

SHE was singing softly to herself the next morning as she stepped out of the shower.

Then she stopped and told herself that there were a lot of things still unresolved between her and Alex and it mightn't be appropriate to be so happy yet. But he came in as she stood in the middle of the bathroom, wearing only a towel and a smile of sheer contentment.

'Well, now, the last time I saw you wearing only a towel I was thwarted by a crisis in the kitchen,' he said with a lazy smile, and drew the towel away.

'Don't remind me!' She wrinkled her nose and realised he was dressed already, in a white business shirt, dark green tie and charcoal trousers. 'Uh…I'll have the towel back, thanks, Alex.'

'Why?'

She looked down at herself. 'You might not have noticed this but I feel a little undressed in comparison to you.'

'Oh, I noticed it,' he said softly. 'I also heard you singing.'

She grimaced. 'I often sing in the shower.'

'Really?' He lifted an eyebrow. 'So it had nothing to do with what transpired last night?'

'Um…' She chewed her lip. 'Perhaps a bit.' She reached for the towel but he withheld it from her. 'Alex!'

'Only a bit?'

She paused and looked at him with a glint in her eyes. 'What do I have to say to get myself out of the bathroom so that I can cook your breakfast—we did agree we were both starving, having missed dinner last night—and so that you can go to work, which you also told me you truly regretted but it was a necessity?'

'Instead of saying anything, why don't we have some really red-hot sex?'

Tattie frowned. 'I thought you disapproved of that?'

'Not any more. The thought of it with you,' he said softly, 'is more than I can bear.'

'Why did you get dressed, then?'

'I have not the faintest idea.' He pulled off his tie and started to unbutton his shirt.

'I've just had a shower,' Tattie said.

'So have I. But I have the solution to that.' He pulled his shirt off and unbuckled his belt. 'The perfect solution.' And he pulled her into his arms.

Tattie took a shaken little breath. There was so much wicked vitality in his eyes. There was so much about him that was just glorious. The tanned width of his shoulders, his height, the springy dark hair of his chest, the washboard stomach and compact hips, the length and strength of his legs. And memories of the night before began to wash through her...

Memories that caused her to tremble finely all over with the knowledge that no part of her slender body was safe from him and the most intense pleasure of his imprint upon it. It was dangerous, it was exciting, and it was heady to think that she could do the same for him. By the time he'd got rid of his trousers it was not only a heady thought but a reality.

'Oh.' She breathed it into words. 'This is living dangerously, I think.'

He looked into her eyes and slid his fingers between her thighs.

She rocked against him, holding his upper arms, and tilted her head back. 'If you kissed me at the same time,' she murmured, 'I'd really like that.'

'My pleasure.' His mouth closed on hers as his fingers continued to ready her for him with the lightest touch, until she gasped that she was dying of joy. Then he crushed her to him and took her in the moments left to them before they climaxed.

He looked into her stunned eyes and brought her back to earth with gentle humour. 'Vertical sex—we are living dangerously, Tattie. Either that or you've turned me a little crazy. But you must admit I couldn't have chosen a better spot to be a bit crazy.' And he lifted her off her feet, carried her to the shower and turned on the water.

For the first few moments Tattie spluttered and wriggled, then she started to laugh and he was laughing with her as water streamed off them.

They finally had breakfast on the veranda.

A slap-up meal of bacon and eggs, grilled tomato, toast—and champagne and orange juice.

'Here's to you.' Alex raised his glass to her. 'My lovely lover.'

Tattie picked up her glass and touched his with it. 'I am without words.'

He grinned. 'That's most unusual.'

'I'll probably recover.'

'Don't doubt it.' He pushed his plate away. 'What are your plans for the day?'

'I have no idea! Why?'

'I'd just like to be able to picture what you're doing while I'm slaving over a hot desk.'

'Oh! Well, I'll probably go out and do some shopping.' Tattie put her knife and fork together. 'Unless—' her eyes widened '—does it show?'

He sat back with his glass and took his time. She wore slim white trousers and a blue and white striped T-shirt. Her hair was tied back in a scrunchie, her feet were bare and she wore no make-up, but her skin glowed.

'Yes.'

She blushed. 'How?'

'There's a new radiance and lustre about you.'

She grew even hotter, and to counteract it said a shade tartly, 'Do you always think in terms of pearls?'

He raised his eyebrows consideringly. 'Can I help it if you remind me of a pearl of the first water?'

'Look...' She laughed a little. 'I'm flattered, but I think you may be flirting with the truth, Alex.'

He moved his shoulders. 'Flirting with something. You. But if you'd rather I got serious?'

'I would.'

'It may be obvious to me, Tattie, but you don't need to worry that it's printed all over you. On the other hand, does it matter?'

Tattie sobered. 'I suppose not. I'd just like this to be between you and me for a while, Alex. I guess I don't have to tell you it's been rather special for me...but it's a very private kind of "special".'

His dark gaze had narrowed, but now it softened. 'All right.' He pushed his chair back and stood up. 'I'm sorry about this, Tattie, but I haven't been into the office for five days now. I'll get home as soon as I can, though.'

He came round to her and drew her to her feet. 'Take care of yourself,' he said softly, and kissed her brow. 'Nor do you have any idea how hard this is to do, I suspect.'

She nestled against him for a moment then looked up

into his eyes. For once they were completely serious and she felt shaken to the core. 'I will,' she murmured huskily.

They had a week.

And Alex spent most of it with her.

They made love when the mood took them. He flew her to Cooinda in Kakadu for the day and they hired a dinghy to explore the wonders of the Yellow Water wetlands on a tributary of the South Alligator River. Even used to Beaufort and Carnarvon as she was, Yellow Water was entrancing for Tattie. This oasis of birdlife, paperbark gums, the lush colours of the billabongs and swamps of the World Heritage listed area in the midst of the sometimes harsh landscape of the Northern Territory, all were astonishingly beautiful.

And instead of flying home that night he flew her to one of the many World War Two airstrips around Darwin. This one was on Mount Bundy Station at Adelaide River, and also offered tourist accommodation.

'Thought you might like to see how others do it,' he told her with a lurking smile.

Of course she was vitally interested to see how others did it, but it caused her a little pang to think how far into the recesses of her mind Beaufort had sunk. She'd spoken to Polly several times, and been assured all was going well, and she would never have dreamt of abandoning Irina through this crisis. But she hadn't spoken of Beaufort since she and Alex had become lovers...

All the same, she fell in love with Mount Bundy and they had a wonderful evening. Their gracious hostess, Fran, suggested they make a party of all the guests and have dinner in the garden of the Adelaide River Tavern, which turned out to be a unique experience, since the buffalo Paul Hogan had "tamed" in *Crocodile Dundee* had lived out its days as a pet at Adelaide River, and was now stuffed in all his glory and took pride of place on top of the bar.

'I don't know why,' Tattie confided to Alex when they were back in their luxurious room at the Mount Bundy homestead, 'but I feel Beaufort lacks something—it could be a stuffed buffalo or, better still, a tame one!'

Alex, at the time, was engaged in undressing her. He paused from this self-appointed task with her blouse in his hands, and withdrew his gaze from her breasts cupped in white lace to look thoughtful.

'I've got buffalo, but I would hesitate to try and do a Crocodile Dundee on any of them. Unless,' he continued, 'you see it as some sort of medieval test you require me to perform for your…favours?'

The last bit was said as he slipped her bra straps down and traced his fingers across the tops of her breasts.

She took a breath. He was sitting on the bed and she was standing between his legs, now only wearing her shorts and underwear.

'That's an idea,' she said gravely. She reached into her pocket and withdrew a clean blue hanky. 'I could even give you this to take into battle with you, tucked into your…helmet or whatever.'

'I suspect I might look a bit silly with it tucked into my helmet.' He took the hanky. 'I could wear it next to my heart, though.'

'It needs to show,' Tattie objected. 'Everyone needs to know that you're performing this dangerous deed for me!'

He tucked the hanky between two buttons of his shirt.

'There. How many people are you planning to invite to my possible demolition by a two-tonne buffalo?'

She gestured widely. 'Heaps. But I have great faith in you, Alex!'

'You do realise Charlie was tame before Paul Hogan got to him?'

She looked down at him, her cornflower-blue eyes alight with laughter. 'I realise a lot of things. A couple of them are that you don't have to go about taming buffalo for my favours, all you have to do is touch me.'

'Like this?' He unclipped her bra, slid it off, abandoned it and spread his hands around her waist. 'I can nearly span this.'

'Mmm,' she agreed. 'Or like this.' And she cupped the back of his head and drew him towards her.

The result was predictable. Before long they were both naked, and he was sculpting her body with his hands and she was shivering in joyful anticipation of his possession of her.

But he paused suddenly, and looked into her eyes. 'What's the other one?'

She blinked. 'Other what?'

'You said there were a couple of things you realised.'

'Oh, that. It doesn't matter.'

'It matters to me, Tattie.'

She looked mischievously stubborn. 'You can't force me to tell you.'

'Yes, I can.' Her arms were around his shoulders and he released them, took her wrists in one hand and positioned them above her head. And he commenced the most devastating assault on her most sensitive spots until she was arching her body in mindless, exquisite desire.

'All right,' she gasped, 'but only after this is over. Alex, I need you!'

'Promise?'

'Yes!'

'Good, because I'm dying here.' He released her wrists and claimed her powerfully.

'This is a little embarrassing,' she said when they'd come down from the heights. 'It's only my opinion, you see.'

He kissed the corner of her mouth. 'Go on. You did promise.'

She moved her cheek on the pillow, her hair spread out in marvellous disarray, and he pulled the sheet over them. 'I was in no position to do anything else,' she told him severely, then laughed softly. 'OK, here goes; I was thinking that I'd taken to this like a duck to water, but again that's only my—'

'You have.'

'My reading of things— I have?'

'Well…' he temporised until she cast him a fierce blue look. 'I can think of a much better analogy, that's all,' he finished with his lips quirking.

'Oh?'

'Uh-huh. A beautiful girl passing into womanhood like a perfect rosebud opening.'

'Alex.' She went to sit up but he pulled her into his arms. 'That's—'

'A bit flowery?' he asked wryly.

They were only inches apart. 'Awesome,' she whispered with her heart in her eyes for a moment. Then she closed them. 'Even if it's not entirely true, I'll cherish those words—'

'Would you like me to show you how true they are?'

Her lashes flew up and her eyes were suddenly wary.

'N-now?' she stammered. 'I don't think I could survive that again. I mean, so soon. I mean—'

He stopped her by kissing her, although he was laughing at the same time. 'If it's any consolation, neither could I. I think we might have done our dash tonight.'

She relaxed and snuggled up against him. She was almost asleep as he stroked her hair, then he said quietly, 'Why did you want me to think there was another man in your life, Tattie? I know now there hasn't been. Not like this anyway.'

She came awake with a slightly chill feeling. 'That...got out of hand,' she said slowly. 'You were the one who suggested it.'

'And you were the one who ran with it.'

'Not really.'

'You didn't exactly deny it.' His hand was still moving rhythmically on her hair, his arm was still around her, but she couldn't help feeling the peace between them was ever so slightly cracked.

'You have to remember your ex-mistress was around the ridges at the time,' she said. 'I was probably suffering from an inferiority complex.'

He was silent for so long she held her breath. Then, 'So there was no man behind your "very good reason" not to want to stay married to me?'

'No, Alex,' she said straightly. 'It just...got out of hand.'

'Good. Sleep well, Tattie.' He hugged her.

But he fell asleep before she did, as her very good reason for not wanting to stay married to him came back to her.

Because, although she had no doubt that Alex Constantin wanted her now, she still didn't know if he was madly in love with her. He couldn't, for example, have been madly in love with Leonie Falconer. He surely would have married her otherwise.

All the same, she had done this, she reflected as she moved ever so slightly in his arms, then froze in case he woke. But he only pulled her closer and slept on. And it was an entirely different matter extricating herself from a marriage that had not been consummated.

She closed her eyes and prayed that the situation would never arise, but in her heart of hearts knew that he was still an enigma to her.

Breakfast at Mount Bundy was bountiful, and Tattie did her best to do it justice as well as conceal from all and sundry that her night's sleep had been patchy.

But something happened as they were setting off to fly back to Darwin that brought her hope.

She was bending over to shake a stone out of her shoe, and when she straightened and turned it was to find Alex standing stock-still behind her with a newly familiar glint in his eye.

She looked him a slightly cautious question, and his teeth flashed in a wry grin.

'You bend over delightfully, Tattie.'

Some colour came to her cheeks, and all she could say was, 'Oh.'

He flicked a careless finger against her hot cheek. 'Don't look so surprised. Did you really think this only went on behind closed doors?'

'Well.' She hesitated. He was reaching up to put a bag into the wing locker of the light plane, there was a slight breeze blowing and it was flattening the thin cotton of his shirt against the long muscles of his back. For a moment she was transfixed at the grace and power of his tall body. Then her sense of fun came to her rescue.

'Well,' she said again, 'despite earlier claims I might have made, Alex, I'm a bit of a newcomer to all this.'

He laughed. 'Then you'd better get used to the idea of me visualising you without your clothes—in all sorts of circumstances.'

She swallowed, and this time her whole body felt hot. 'Uh—does that mean I'm not altogether safe, even on this plane?'

'You may not be safe,' he agreed gravely, then relented as her eyes nearly popped. 'Safe from my thoughts. In all other respects I'm a very conscientious pilot.'

'Thank heavens!' She started to laugh. 'You had me worried for a moment.'

'Since you've converted me to red-hot sex, I wouldn't count on always being safe, Tattie,' he murmured as he closed the locker and took her in his arms.

'I converted you! That is a supreme misrepresentation of the facts,' she protested.

'Whatever,' he said softly, with his eyes dancing wickedly, and he subjected her to a long, leisurely but supremely effective kiss.

'I just hope there was no one watching,' she said in a husky undertone when he'd done his worst and was tidying her up—smoothing her hair and straightening the collar of her blouse.

He smiled like the devil and kissed the tip of her nose. 'I don't give a damn how many people were watching. Shall we go home?'

As they flew the short distance to Darwin Airport Tattie examined her feelings.

She discovered she felt more reassured, as if the ripple in their relationship last night, like a cat's paw on the surface of a fish pond, had smoothed over again. Then she found that she felt more than reassured; she felt positively jaunty. Was that the result, she pondered, of having a man fantasise about you without your clothes in all sorts of circumstances, particularly a man like Alex? As a confidence-booster it was rather unique, she acknowledged.

Naturally, it still did not answer the question of whether he was madly in love with her, she cautioned herself, but it made her feel incredibly good...

'Penny for them?' Alex broke into her thoughts.

'No way, not this time!'

He raised an eyebrow at her. Then, as if he understood what had been going through her mind, he put his hand over hers and said no more. And that, Tattie discovered, was the most reassuring thing of all.

Two days later she spoke to Natalie at Beaufort and was able to pass on the news that Irina was doing well and would be out of hospital shortly.

'That's such good news, Tatiana,' Natalie said down the line.

'Yes, it's wonderful. How are things there?'

'Going extremely well, darling. But there's just one thing. Doug and I have to go back to Perth next weekend. He's got an exhibition coming up and he really needs to be there. I would also love to be there. Do you think, now that Irina's so much better, you could come back to Beaufort?'

'Of course. Well...' Tattie hesitated. 'Even if I can't I'll make some arrangements—you go ahead, Mum.'

'Tattie—'

'Don't argue, Mum,' Tattie said humorously down the

line. 'Between us, Alex and I will come up with something.'

'How are…things with you and Alex?' Natalie enquired a little diffidently.

'Fine,' Tattie said brightly.

'Is he there with you, listening, perhaps?'

Sensing that her mother was about to embark on an in-depth discussion of her marriage, Tattie told a lie. 'Yes, as a matter of fact.'

'Oh, well.' Natalie recouped. 'Give him my regards, my sweet.' And not long afterwards they ended the call.


'My mother sends you her regards.'

Alex looked up from the documents he was reading. He'd been to work for a few hours and brought a pile of papers home with him. They were currently spread all over the coffee-table in the den. Tattie had made them afternoon tea and was sitting curled up in a chair, reading.

'Via mental telepathy?' he asked, looking amused.

Tattie wrinkled her nose at him. 'No. She rang while you were at work.'

'What else did she have to say?' He returned to the documents and sorted them into a different order.

At the same time Tattie examined her reluctance to bring up the subject of her returning to Beaufort, although she knew she had no choice.

She said, 'Doug has an exhibition opening in Perth this weekend. They want to be there for it.' But she wasn't sure, as she said it, whether the fact that she now had his undivided attention was a good thing or not.

'So. Are you all set to hotfoot it back to Beaufort, Tattie?'

*Not* a good thing, his undivided attention, she decided,

nor the fact that she couldn't read his expression at all. She closed her book and swung her bare feet to the floor. 'Alex, of course not—unless you can come with me—'

'I'm afraid that's out of the question at the moment.'

'Because of your mother? I can fully understand—'

'That and business commitments.' His tone was clipped and curt.

She opened her hands in a helpless little gesture. 'But the thing is, I just can't leave Polly to cope with a houseful of guests.'

'The thing is,' he parodied, 'we now need to make different arrangements for Beaufort.'

She swallowed. 'Naturally, I realise some things will have to change—'

'Yes, they will, Tattie. From now on you belong here.'

She stared into his determined dark eyes and couldn't believe this was the man she now slept with so joyfully. How could he go from that to this rising sense of anger that was about to escape?

'Don't take that tone with me, Alex Constantin,' she said grimly. 'If we can't discuss this rationally then there's no point in discussing it at all. It was never my intention to run Beaufort from Darwin and...it was you yourself who suggested the whole thing in the first place and told me how I would be the one to hold it all together—I can't just walk away from it!'

'You don't agree that your place is here?' he shot back dangerously.

'Yes. No.' She shut her eyes in sheer frustration. 'I put my heart and soul into getting the tourist operation off the ground and I intend to see it through. *Of course* I'll have to make some adjustments, but why can't we both make the necessary adjustments? Why do I have to be *told* where my place is like a…a chattel? Or a partner in an arranged marriage?'

'I would have thought,' he drawled in a way that made him even more dangerous, 'it was a requirement even for marriages made in heaven to live together.'

'It is! That doesn't mean to say some exceptions can't be made for certain circumstances. That doesn't mean to say you can order me around and refuse to have a sensible discussion—'

'I have the perfect couple in mind to put in place on Beaufort. They've had previous experience—they ran a lodge adjacent to Litchfield National Park—'

'Listen to me, Alex,' she broke in, now truly incensed. 'I will make any decisions regarding that kind of thing!'

'So this isn't a marriage belatedly but nevertheless made in heaven?'

'Not if you're going to treat me like this.' She dashed at some angry tears.

'As a matter of interest, Tattie, what means more to you—me or Beaufort and Carnarvon?'

'It's not a question of that!' she protested.

He looked at her cynically. Then he shuffled his papers together and stood up. 'I think I'll go back to work.'

'Why don't you?' she whispered with her throat working and an awful sense of desolation in her heart. And some demon prompted her to add tearfully, 'Just don't stop by any pub where your father is likely to be watching rugby. That's the last thing I need, more family intervention.'

She was asleep when he came home that night, and she stayed in her bedroom until she heard him leave the next morning—but she hadn't locked her door.

She might have been emotionally exhausted and devastated at the minefield her marriage had become, but one small part of her had hoped for a miracle. That he would come to her and they would sort through it all. It was such a small issue, she reasoned. Or was it? Surely he could see that she couldn't suddenly abandon a project so close to her heart?

Nothing in the preceding five days had given her to suspect he would be a law-laying-down husband—the opposite, if anything. But the supreme irony of that was how misplaced her sense of jaunty self-confidence in relation to her powers of attracting him had been—she cringed inwardly at the thought.

Finally, she got up, and knew she needed to get out. With not the slightest interest in how she looked, she pulled on a pair of fawn shorts, a big white linen over-blouse with patch pockets and a pair of white sand shoes. She tied her hair back severely, abjured all make-up and hid her eyes behind a large pair of sunglasses. Then she drove her Golf down to Cullen Bay for a late breakfast.

Cullen Bay was the trend-setter in recent marina development in Darwin. Because of huge tide variations, conventional marinas had not been a possibility on the Darwin Harbour foreshores until someone had come up with the idea of building locks to enclose the marinas. At Cullen Bay there was much more—apartments and town houses overlooking the marina, shops and restaurants. It was always a bustling, lively place, and Tattie chose her favourite café and her favourite spot where she could look over all the yachts moored at the jetties.

She ordered coffee and raisin toast. She wasn't feeling hungry, but there was an aching hollow within her that some food might just appease.

At the same time as her order arrived, however, so

did the last person on the planet she wanted to see—
Leonie Falconer.

Moreover, Alex's ex-mistress pulled out a chair and
sat down.

Tattie straightened. 'What—?'

'I was watching you; I've just had a late breakfast
myself,' Leonie said. 'You…looked a bit pensive, so I
thought I'd saunter over and ask you how it's going.
Alex behaving himself?' she asked blandly.

If this wasn't bad enough, Tattie thought darkly,
Leonie was looking glorious. In a skimpy cherry-red little top that revealed her midriff—and a silver navel-
stud—together with a short hot-pink chiffon skirt, she
was colourful, and not a lot of her full golden figure was
left to the imagination. Her long hair was casually
wound up, she wore some stunning rings on her slender
hands and her air of confidence was not to be doubted.

Tattie couldn't help glancing down at herself—in contrast she was about as colourful and confident-looking
as a mouse. She had to call on all her Beaufort spirit…
She picked up her coffee-cup and said over the rim,
'He's behaving beautifully, Leonie! Thank you so much
for asking.'

Her tormentor's hazel eyes narrowed. 'I thought you
looked a bit down in the mouth, to be honest, Tatiana.'

'How acute of you!' Tattie marvelled. 'I am, but only
because I'm going to have to leave Alex for a few days.
One of my cattle stations needs me.'

Leonie sat back, and Tattie thought—Take that, Ms
Falconer!

'You know,' Leonie murmured, 'over the past few
months—well, the whole course of your marriage, in
fact—I've wondered how well you know Alex
Constantin.'

'Strange you should say that—other people have said the same to me—but I know him very well indeed. Very well.' Better than I want to know him right now, Tattie added, but to herself.

'So you were quite comfortable with him sleeping with me while you were married?' Leonie queried.

Tattie shrugged. 'Since I recommended he go out and get himself a mistress, why not?'

She saw the little flare of shock in Leonie's eyes and thought, Bingo again!—then flinched inwardly and wondered what she thought she was doing.

But Leonie had regrouped. 'And you know all about Flora Simpson?'

If she'd been angry with Alex yesterday it was nothing to what was building up inside her now, Tattie discovered, and assured herself she couldn't be responsible for what she said at this moment. 'Bless her heart, yes! A two-timing hussy, by the sound of it.'

'Perhaps,' Leonie responded, but she was pale around the mouth. 'But are you quite prepared to accept that he'll never get over her? I suppose you do know she's newly back in town and she's divorced her husband?' She leant forward and added with malice aforethought, 'Don't think that the whole of Darwin doesn't know why he married you—because he couldn't have her and it didn't matter who the hell he married, Tatiana Beaufort.'

'Constantin, actually. Do they? Ah, well, that's life.' She sipped her coffee just in case she was tempted to pour it all over Leonie Falconer. 'But, you know, if that's the case I can't help wondering why he didn't marry you.'

Leonie paled all over her face. 'Because you had one thing I didn't—cattle stations. That's all he married you for.'

Tattie stood up and grinned. 'That's two things actually. But let's not split hairs. And I have to confess he has a few…assets that appeal to me. Good day to you.'

She drove, without thinking, to the legal-aid office where she'd given her time so often during the first year of her marriage. But after she'd parked the car she decided she might as well go in and say hello. Anything to take the bitter taste of Leonie Falconer out of her mouth.

One of her favourite solicitors was on duty, and for once the office wasn't busy, so she sat down opposite Jenny Jones and had a chat. Jenny was in her thirties, and adopted a hippie style of dress—long, trailing skirts and fringed waistcoats—but she possessed a shrewd brain and boundless humanity.

'Anything interesting going on?' Tattie asked.

Jenny shrugged. 'Mostly the usual. By the way, Laura Pearson has had her baby—a boy. But it's a bit sad— her boyfriend has run out on her.'

Laura Pearson had been a legal secretary in the office, a girl Tattie had always liked, and she asked Jenny for her address so she could take her a present.

Jenny fished it out. 'How's life on the station treating you, Tattie? I must say, we miss you here.'

'Fine. Jen,' Tattie said as the thought came to her out of the blue, 'how would you go about tracking down someone?'

Jenny looked surprised. 'Why?'

'I just…would like to trace someone I've…lost track of,' Tattie improvised.

'Well, you could try the electoral rolls.'

Tattie grimaced. 'I believe she's just moved back to Darwin, so she might not yet be in the telephone book or on the rolls.'

'Hmm… You said—moved back to Darwin.' Jenny chewed her pen for a moment. 'Was she socially prominent before she left, or anything like that?'

'She might have been,' Tattie said slowly.

'You could try the local newspaper. They might have got wind of her return. I'll give you the name of a journalist I know there.'

Half an hour later Tattie left the legal-aid office with a name on a slip of paper in her pocket. But she was not at all sure of the wisdom of Tatiana Constantin going into a newspaper office and requesting any information they might have in their back files on one Flora Simpson.

All the same, thanks to Leonie and her venom, she now had an almost overwhelming desire to see clearly this shadowy figure who two people had intimated might have been the love of Alex's life—two people, above all, who should know.

She was staring, preoccupied, into a shop window when she realised it was a toy shop with a most delightful dancing teddy bear in the window. So she went in and bought it for Laura Pearson's baby, then had an amazing thought.

Accordingly she found another shop and bought herself a hat, one that she could pull down on her head and hide a lot of her face beneath its floppy brim. Then she marched into the office of the local newspaper and told the receptionist she had come from the legal-aid office on behalf of Jenny Jones, who would be very grateful if they could check their back files for anything on Flora Simpson.

It took a while, but it worked. No one appeared to recognise her, and she only dealt with the receptionist because Jenny's name worked like magic. She left even-

tually with an envelope she didn't attempt to open until
she got home.

There was no sign of Alex as she pulled off her con-
cealing hat. All the same, she locked herself in her bedroom to study the contents of the envelope. Then she
wished she hadn't been so cunning as she studied photos
of her nemesis. For Flora Simpson had all the allure of
a truly beautiful woman.

There was not the earthy golden attraction of Leonie
Falconer, but there was something more ethereal about
her, although she was tall and fair. There was not only
grace and a lovely figure, but also composure and intelligence.

She let the photos flutter to the bed, then forced herself to read the couple of cuttings that had accompanied
them. One of them told her that Flora had returned to
her home town of Darwin after her divorce from her
wealthy financier husband about two weeks ago.

How old would she be? she wondered. And judged
her to be in her late twenties or early thirties. So, not
only stunning, she reflected with her eyes squeezed shut,
but also much closer to Alex in age and maturity. She
tidied the photos back into the envelope and hid them
at the back of her wardrobe.

The phone rang. She picked up the extension on her
bedside table.

It was Alex with a bad connection, a strong hum in
the background. 'Tattie?'

'Yes? Where are you?'

'On a plane; something has come up and I'm flying
out to one of the pearl farms, but I should be back tomorrow.'

'All right.' She cleared her throat. 'Alex, I'm glad you
rang—just in case you thought I'd been kidnapped, I'm

going back to Beaufort tomorrow. I'll see your mother this afternoon to explain why I have to go back—'

'Tattie, don't,' he said abruptly.

'Alex, I have to.' And she put the phone down. It rang again almost immediately but she ignored it. And half an hour later she ignored another call.

She soon discovered that Alex Constantin was not the right person to ignore, however. She got ready to visit Irina in hospital that afternoon, only to discover a huge young man outside her front door, who politely informed her that he was a security guard and he'd been instructed not to let her out of his sight.

A flicker of fear and the memory of Parap came to her and she stepped back inside smartly, saying she would just like to check it out.

She leant back against the door, trying to regulate her breathing, before she rang Alex on his satellite phone. There was no reply, so she tried his secretary, Paula Gibbs.

'Oh, Mrs Constantin,' Paula said, relieved, 'I was just coming over to visit you. I tried to call you but got no answer.'

'Oh. Paula, what on earth is going on? There's someone who claims to be a security guard outside my door.'

'He is a security guard.' Paula went on to explain how Alex had been called away unexpectedly and how he'd rung her from the plane and asked her to organise it.

'But...but has something happened I'm not aware of?' Tattie asked.

'Not at *all*,' Paula stressed. 'It's just that—I guess because it nearly happened once Alex would feel happier about leaving you alone with him in place. That's why I tried to ring you, so you'd know what was going on. He's from our own security team, incidentally.'

Tattie took a deep breath and counted to ten beneath her breath. 'OK. Thanks, Paula.' She put the phone down and once more sallied forth through her front door, where she advised her guardian angel that he'd better prepare himself for a trip to a cattle station in the Kimberley tomorrow.

He looked embarrassed, but replied that he had instructions not to let her leave Darwin until Mr Constantin returned. For her own safety, of course, he added.

She restrained herself from explaining to him that the only issue at stake here was her husband's diabolical determination to have his own way, although couched in much less formal language, and did the only thing she could—went to see her mother-in-law with the large young man squeezed uncomfortably into her Golf.

# CHAPTER NINE

'WHAT'S your name?' Tattie asked as she steered the Golf.

'Leroy, ma'am.'

'Well, Leroy, could I ask you to stop cracking your knuckles?'

'Sorry, ma'am.' He squashed his hands beneath him.

'What will you do while I'm visiting my mother-in-law?'

'Just stand outside the door, ma'am,' he said reassuringly. 'You won't even know I'm around.'

His sheer bulk made this highly unlikely, Tattie thought drily.

'And tonight?'

'Same thing, but my colleague will take over at midnight. There are two of us assigned to you, Mrs Constantin, so you have absolutely nothing to worry about.'

Tattie flicked him a glance. He had a broad, ruddy face beneath fair curly hair and small blue eyes. But he looked genuinely prepared to defend her to the nth degree while being as nice and polite about it as he could, and she couldn't help feeling a bit sorry for him. For, little though Leroy knew it, his problems were going to lie in the opposite direction...

By hook or by crook she was going to get herself to Beaufort before Alex came home!

\* \* \*

Irina was sitting up in a beautiful pink and cream silk bed jacket.

Tattie kissed her and sat down beside the bed. 'You're looking wonderful,' she told her mother-in-law.

'I'm beginning to feel human at last,' Irina replied. 'And they say I will walk out of here—maybe on a walking frame for a time, but walk all the same.'

'I know you will!'

Irina patted her face. 'You've been so sweet to me, Tattie! And I only thank my lucky stars that Alex had you by his side through all this.'

Tattie studied the pearl-encrusted pewter vase beside the bed with a fresh spray of orchids in it. 'He loves you so much. So do I. But...' She hesitated. 'I have to go away for a few days—just to Beaufort.' And she explained the situation.

Irina beamed at her. 'I think it's just wonderful that your mother has found someone to love. So romantic. She brought him to meet me, you know. In fact, I bought one of his paintings. I do hope he has a successful exhibition. How long will you be gone, my dear?'

*I would love to know how much you know, Irina, and what Alex told you when I ran away to Beaufort,* Tattie thought. Because she felt as if she was walking on eggshells, and ten times more so because Irina was in hospital and had nearly died.

'I'm not sure,' she said. 'Alex knows of a couple who could take over now I've got the project off the ground.' She paused. 'I haven't met them, but from the forward bookings we have I think it is going to be a success and I'm...*really* happy about that.'

Irina studied her thoughtfully. 'You know, we all underestimated you, Tattie.'

Tattie blinked in surprise.

'And perhaps most of all Alex did,' Irina went on. 'Would I be correct in saying you're not prepared to accept anything but true love from Alex?'

Tattie almost fell off her chair, and Irina smiled wisely. 'Everyone thinks I'm a silly old woman who imagines her only son can do no wrong. And, yes, perhaps I did have to have it pointed out to me who Leonie Falconer was—too late, as it happened.'

'Who...?' Tattie stared at her dazedly.

'A friend of mine rang me the day after the anniversary party. I don't know if you remember, but that's why I rang you the next morning in a bit of a state.'

'Yes,' Tattie breathed as her mind flew backwards. 'Oh!'

Irina patted her hand again. 'And now they tell me Flora Simpson is back in town.'

Such was her surprise, Tattie was speechless for almost a minute. 'But...you weren't supposed to know about her!'

'The only amusing aspect of that, Tattie,' Irina said a shade ruefully, 'is that both George and I knew but we tried to shield each other from the knowledge.'

Tattie gazed at her helplessly.

'Of course you must do as you see fit, Tattie; I suspect you've done that all the way through,' Irina continued. 'But only you can know what's best for you in regard to Alex. If half a loaf is not good enough for you, then stick to your guns, my dear. I did.'

'I... This... You mean with George? But I thought that yours was an arranged marriage and you approved of that kind of thing.'

'Firstly, yes—I mean George. Although it wasn't quite the same situation as you and Alex. He might have thought his mother arranged our marriage but what he didn't know was that I planted the seeds of it in his mother's mind. I wanted George, you see, but he couldn't quite make up his mind about me.' Irina gazed fondly back down the years. 'Now he's quite convinced *he* made the right choice, with a little help from his mother.'

'Bravo, Mama Constantin!' Tattie said softly, using the pet name Alex sometimes used for his mother.

Irina smiled. 'As for arranged marriages in general, all I ever wanted to do was find a girl Alex could fall in love with, or, if not that, grow to love and respect. Instead, I found a girl *I* will always love and admire, whatever happens between her and my son. Of course, I hope and pray that you and Alex will resolve your differences, but that is not my main concern now. A little brush with death,' she said humorously, 'gives you a new perspective on life, I think. Be happy for yourself, Tattie.' And she leant forward to put her arms around Tattie.

'On the other hand,' she said softly as she cupped Tattie's face, 'I predict he will not give a damn about Flora Simpson being back in town.'

Back home in the apartment, Tattie tried to sort through this surprise development as well as she could.

It was an intense relief, she realised, not to be hiding things from her mother-in-law any more. It was even more of a relief to know that she had been vindicated in a sense, or at least had had her side of the story understood by his mother and was still loved and admired just for herself. So what was the fly in the ointment? she wondered.

How could anyone predict what Alex's reaction to the beautiful Flora Simpson would be. That was one of them. As for fly two, she thought with a grim spark of humour, it was quite simple. She refused to be dictated to by her husband. If he truly loved her, as opposed to finding her desirable at the moment, surely he would have been prepared to discuss the situation at Beaufort rather than simply laying down the law?

She glanced towards the front door. Surely he wouldn't subject her to what virtually amounted to imprisonment just to get his own way?

She chewed her knuckles for a while, then came to a decision. She made her plans, which included a phone call, then got out the dancing teddy bear she'd bought earlier in the day and wrapped it up. She took a cup of tea and some shortbread out to Leroy—she had already provided him with a chair.

'Thank you very much, ma'am!' Leroy said enthusiastically.

'By the way, Leroy, I'm going out to dinner at a friend's house in about an hour. Do you have your own transport?'

Leroy hesitated.

'I only ask because it could be uncomfortable for you to be sitting in the Golf for a few hours, so perhaps you'd like to chauffeur me backwards and forwards in your car, if it's bigger?'

Leroy's face cleared. 'My Holden is bigger, if you wouldn't mind?'

'Not at all! See you soon.'

'Where are we going?' Leroy asked an hour later as he ushered Tattie into the front seat of his Holden.

She gave him an address in Fannie Bay, then enquired what he intended to do for dinner, because her visit might take a good couple of hours.

'I was going to ask you if you'd mind if I stopped to get a burger, ma'am.'

'Please do, Leroy. I'd hate to think of you sitting there for hours, starving.'

So they stopped at a drive-thru, where he ordered an inordinate amount of food, then drove to Fannie Bay.

'This is it.' Tattie pointed to a house, although she'd never seen it before.

Leroy parked in the driveway and looked around alertly. 'Don't you worry, Mrs Constantin. I'll do regular checks to make sure the house and grounds are secure, and here's my mobile number just in case you need me.' He handed her a card.

Not too regular, Tattie prayed, and felt a trickle of guilt. Then she stiffened her spine, thanked him, and went to visit Laura Pearson and her new baby.

Laura was thrilled to see her, and thrilled with the present, although the baby, at two months, was unimpressed. 'Just wait until he's a little older, Tattie, I'm sure he'll adore it. Let's have a cup of tea.'

So they had tea and a little chat, then the baby started to protest. 'He's hungry—he's always hungry,' Laura said ruefully, with a spark of exhaustion in her eyes.

'Well, don't worry about me, Laura. I can let myself out. You just sit down with him and put your feet up. What can I get you? Aren't nursing mums supposed to drink gallons of water? I'll get you a glass.'

And it was as easy as that. Tattie settled Laura and the baby in a comfortable chair, put some nice music on for her and brought her a glass of water. Then she said goodbye and took the tea things back to the kitchen on her way out.

'I'll just go out the back way,' she called softly, and did so.

But instead of heading for the drive and Leroy, after a short, pregnant reconnaissance she tiptoed across the back lawn, climbed the low fence into the house behind Laura's, prayed she wouldn't be set upon by vicious dogs or vigilant householders, and stole out onto the street behind.

Then she started to walk rapidly away, thinking that the only thing that could go wrong would be if Laura noted that she hadn't heard a car start up. She would just have to take a gamble on the girl being too involved with her baby. She pulled her mobile phone from her bag and called a taxi. Within twenty minutes she was in the garage of her apartment building, driving the Golf out of it. And ten minutes later, when she was sure she was far enough away from home not to be found easily, she called Paula Gibbs on her home phone number.

'Mrs Constantin.' Paula drew a shaky breath. 'Alex will—'

'Paula, all you have to do is tell Alex I'm going to Beaufort, come hell or high water,' Tattie said firmly. 'I'm perfectly safe, I promise you. But what you need to do *right* now is call Leroy off. I don't want my friend hassled in any way, and I mean that! Nor is it Leroy's fault in *any* way; I deliberately gave him the slip.'

'But...but...why?' Paula objected.

'It's just something between me and Alex, Paula. Incidentally, don't even think of calling the police, because that would create the kind of gossip Alex would *hate*. And please don't bother his father; he's got enough on his plate at the moment.'

'How are you getting to Beaufort?'

'I'm flying. Bye now, Paula!'

*    *    *

Two days later Tattie arrived at Beaufort in a light plane she'd chartered.

She'd driven to Katherine and had to spend the night there. She'd left the Golf in a garage and taken a Greyhound bus to Kununurra, from where she'd chartered the light plane after another night in a motel. She was almost reeling from physical tiredness and mental exhaustion as she stepped out of it onto the airstrip, and was immensely relieved to see no other plane on the strip. The last thing she felt like doing was confronting Alex.

But there was a surprise waiting for her. Polly drove down to the strip, as was the custom when the homestead was buzzed by incoming planes. And she flung her arms around Tattie.

'Thank heavens you've arrived! Not only is Alex in a terrible mood, but we've also got a houseful of guests!'

'But what about my mother and Doug? I didn't think they were going until Friday, and I didn't think…you had…any bookings.' Tattie's voice ran down as the other pertinent bit of information sank in. 'You mean Alex is here?' She stared at Polly disbelievingly.

'Hop in.' Polly gestured to the four-wheel-drive vehicle. 'I'll explain on the way.'

She did. Alex had arrived yesterday morning straight from the pearl farm, in a combination float and wheel plane. He'd sent her mother and Doug to Darwin in it, so they could get a flight to Perth, and told them that she, Tattie, was on her way to Beaufort. Then, out of the blue, a bus-load of tourists had arrived with confirmed bookings for two nights' accommodation.

'But…how…?'

'Somehow the dates must have got scrambled; we weren't expecting them until next week. Mind you, I had everything hunky-dory, but...' Polly raised her eyebrows expressively. 'Anyway, Alex bucked in and helped. In fact he's taken them on the billabong tour, so Mum and I can concentrate on dinner. But he's been talking to all sorts of people on the phone and, well, it sounded to me as if no one knew where you were, Tattie.'

'I...I was planning to fly from Katherine, but I couldn't get a flight so I had to take the bus to Kununurra.'

Polly drew up in front of the homestead and looked at her strangely. 'You couldn't have hopped on a Constantin plane?'

Tattie swallowed. 'It...got a bit complicated, Polly. Where's Oscar?'

Polly blinked, then shivered suddenly. 'Uh...he's gone with Alex. They should be back in a couple of hours.'

They were the longest few hours of Tattie's life.

Nothing could have been more eloquent or indicative of Alex's state of mind than Polly's involuntary shiver. And nothing gave her hope that the sight of her on the homestead veranda when the billabong tour returned was alleviating her husband's state of mind.

He surveyed her, his expression darkly inscrutable, and if it hadn't been for Oscar a pall would have been thrown over the whole party, she was sure. But Oscar suddenly realised who she was and raced up to her with utter delight palpably displayed all over his body.

She bent down and he jumped into her arms. 'Oh, you've grown, young man! How long have I been away? I don't think we can do this any longer.' She staggered and put the dog down as everyone laughed, and the tension of the moment dissipated. For most of them...

Alex began to introduce her to the party and she was regaled with all the marvels they'd seen. Then he said, 'If you'll excuse us for a moment, folks, my wife and I haven't seen each other for a couple of days. Polly?'

Polly leapt into action and told everyone that afternoon tea would be ready in half an hour.

And Alex's hand descended on Tattie's elbow and he led her off the veranda.

Not far from the homestead they'd built a gazebo on a rise like a small bluff, and the country sloped away from it in a lovely wild valley to a blue ridge.

It was pagoda-shaped, with curved empty embrasures and a wooden lattice half-wall. The floor was paved, but the timber was natural and it blended in well with the country. There were benches to sit on. It was a wonderful place to sit in peace, to watch nature and to feel the vastness of Beaufort.

But Alex said not a word as he escorted Tattie to it, and she had the absolute feeling that peace was not on the agenda. Even Oscar seemed to get the vibes and become subdued.

And, as she climbed the steps, her nerves got the better of her.

'If you've brought me here to have me shot at dawn, Alex,' she said tautly, 'think again!'

She swung round to face him.

He leant his shoulders against an upright and crossed his arms. In jeans and a black shirt he looked dusty, tired, perhaps, but all the same very tough.

In contrast, although she too wore jeans, she was neat and clean in a pink blouse and with her hair smooth and tucked behind her ears.

'Why would I do that, Tattie?'

'Because I disobeyed you, because—'

'You're getting a little emotional and unrealistic here, surely?'

'Am I? I don't think so,' she flung at him. 'You virtually had me imprisoned so you could get your own way, Alex! Look, I'm sorry if I worried you but I will not be dictated to like that!'

'Go on.'

'What more is there to say? But if you want more, you can have it! You expect me to live in a place where I keep falling over your ex-mistresses—'

He straightened. 'When did that happen?'

'It doesn't matter.'

'I think it may, Tattie. Tell me.'

She swallowed but stood her ground as he loomed over her, and refused to speak.

He said evenly, 'All right, that aside, you're rather cavalier with your apologies for what you've put a few people through, Tattie. Paula, for example. She had no way of knowing someone wasn't forcing you to ring her. The security guard—'

'It wasn't his fault,' Tattie broke in. 'It was all your fault for treating me the way you did. And I swear, if there are any repercussions for Leroy over this I will never speak to you again, Alex Constantin.'

He raised a wry eyebrow. 'Your concern for Leroy is touching, Tattie. What about my mother?'

'Your mother? She knew I was coming back to Beaufort, Alex, she just didn't know the lengths I had to go to get here. But for your information, your mother is no longer of the opinion I should stay married to you if I don't want to.'

He frowned. 'Why?'

'She thinks you all underestimated me—you in particular.'

'She told you this?'

'She did,' Tattie agreed. 'With no prompting from me,' she added. 'A brush with mortality did it. She actually told me that if you didn't fit my requirements...' She paused suddenly.

'Which are, Tattie?' he asked very quietly.

'It doesn't matter,' she mumbled as some colour came to her cheeks.

'Once again I beg to differ. Would those requirements have anything to do with the mysterious reason you keep parading before me for not wanting to stay in this marriage?'

His gaze was so intent she felt as if it was pinning her to the gazebo upright she'd involuntarily backed into.

'I can always get those requirements from my mother,' he murmured.

She bit her lip and closed her eyes. 'Alex...' She couldn't go on.

'Tell me, Tattie. I won't let you go until you do.'

She never knew afterwards what unlocked the secret she'd tried so desperately to keep from him, for so long. The bush beyond the gazebo was hot and still, the blue ridge in the distance was swimming in a heat haze, Oscar was lying beside her with his head on his paws but every now and then he was sending her an alert look.

She was in the place she loved best with the man she loved—when she wasn't hating him—perhaps it was the sum of all this that made it impossible for her to dodge and dive any longer.

She licked her lips and everything about Alex she loved came back to her, which was incredibly unfair in the light of his recent behaviour, but none the less all the times he'd made love to her came back beneath the impact of his tall, electrifying presence...

And the words seemed to tumble out of their own accord.

'I swore I would not stay married to you, Alex—' she swallowed painfully '—unless I knew you were madly in love with me.'

'Why not?' His words seemed to echo.

But at the very last moment she couldn't do it. Her throat worked and she blinked away incipient tears. 'The thing is, I understand now.'

'Understand what, Tattie?' He asked it very quietly.

She could see the line on his forehead where his hat had rested, she could breathe in the dust on his clothes and the sweat of an energetic ride, all of it purely masculine and terribly fascinating—but not for her.

'Why you could never fall madly in love with me.' She shrugged in what she hoped was a wry little gesture. 'I've seen Flora Simpson, so—'

*'When?'* he asked dangerously.

Her lips parted and Oscar sat up, growled low in his throat and then looked embarrassed, and bunted them both on the legs to show that he didn't think he'd meant it but he'd be much happier if he didn't have to take sides.

Tattie laughed nervously and patted him. 'It's OK.'

All Alex did was continue to look the question at her.

She sighed. 'Not in the flesh. I saw a...some pictures of her, that's all.'

'How come?'

'I'd rather not tell you that, Alex; it's a bit embarrassing.'

'Let me get this straight. You claimed earlier you'd

been falling all over my ex-mistresses but now it appears it wasn't Flora—not in the flesh at least. I don't get it,' he said flatly.

Tattie squared her shoulders. 'I ran into Leonie the day you left town. She…she told me amongst other things that Flora was back in town. So I…' She closed her eyes frustratedly. 'You have to remember your own father filled me in on how Flora had affected your life, Alex.' Her lashes lifted. 'So I decided I was sick and tired of having this…person hanging over my head.' And she told him how she'd got the pictures of Flora.

'Oh, Tattie.' He said it barely audibly.

'Which is how I came to understand why you could never be madly in love with me. She's…even in a picture she's just special.' Some of her Beaufort hauteur came back to Tattie. 'Although if the reason you wanted to keep me in Darwin was part of some tit-for-tat game you're playing with her, that I cannot admire, Alex,' she said severely.

His lips twisted. 'When did you work that out?'

Tattie looked surprised. 'It's just hit me, actually,' she said uneasily. 'I can't think of any other reason for it.'

'Can't you?' He rested a hand on the curved embrasure above her head. 'I can. All this.' He looked into the distance then his dark eyes came back to her. 'Beaufort, in other words. And Carnarvon. Let's not forget Carnarvon. It has become an abiding nightmare for me.'

'What has?' she whispered, her eyes wide.

'How much more they mean to you than I do. And I'm sorry to have to disillusion you, Tatiana Beaufort…' He paused.

If her eyes were wide before they were now stunned and incredibly confused.

'But I have actually fallen madly in love with you,'

he continued. 'I apologise if it's been a slightly protracted process. If you doubt the authenticity of it, though, I even went to the extreme lengths of virtually locking you up so that you couldn't come here on your own and forget about me while you got all caught up in being here, being a Beaufort and all the rest.'

'Alex…' It was a mere breath of sound.

'Furthermore…' He took his hand away from the embrasure to touch her hair fleetingly, and a nerve flickered in his jaw. 'I had no idea Flora Simpson was back in town but, yes, thanks to her, I didn't really want to fall in love again. It took a girl with so much spirit, so much life, so much about her that brings me joy to change my mind. You, Tattie.'

'But I thought you were so cross with me!'

He shook his head. 'I was so relieved to see you I didn't quite know how I was going to handle myself. I didn't know what was in your heart.'

She gazed at him.

'When Paula rang me two nights ago it was the worst moment of my life.'

'Why?'

He smiled, but not amusedly. 'I thought you might have run away from me for good.'

'Is this…is this all true?' Tattie gasped.

'Tattie,' he said abruptly, 'it only took five days after you first slept with me for you to want to come back here. If I'm a mass of insecurities, can you blame me?'

'A mass of insecurities,' she repeated. 'Alex, if only you *knew*.'

'You could tell me,' he suggested. 'You mentioned something about requirements earlier.'

'Oh. Yes. Yes, well, one of those requirements, as I

told you, was that I needed you to be madly in love with me.'

'Why?' he said simply.

'Because I've been madly in love with you for a long time, Alex, and—'

But she said no more, because he'd pulled her into his arms and she could hear the way his heart was beating, fast and furiously.

'I thought I was never going to get you to say the words,' he said unevenly into her hair. 'It was driving me crazy. Oh, Tattie, I love you, sweetheart.'

'What are we going to do?' Tattie said.

They were sitting side by side on a bench with their arms around each other. Tattie had been gloriously and repeatedly kissed, and had done not a little of her fair share of participating in it.

'About life in general or our particular circumstances of the moment?' he queried.

She moved against him and laid her cheek on his shoulder. 'You know, Alex, one of the reasons Beaufort meant so much to me was because I didn't think I could have you. So long as I can keep coming back here, I'll be happy, but now I've got you—' she glinted a mischievous little look at him '—I won't need to live all my life here.'

'Do you want to keep the tourist enterprise going?'

She thought for a moment. 'Yes. For several reasons. I rather like sharing it with the world. I think beauty in whatever form—music, art, literature, nature—may just help people to understand and cope with life better. But I'd also like to keep it going for Polly and my mother and Doug, and Marie and the blacksmith's wife, who all seem to have a richer life because of this venture. I do have one ulterior motive, though.'

'Let me guess,' he drawled, 'you'd still like to drag Carnarvon out of the red by your own efforts?'

'How did you know?' She gazed at him innocently.

'You forget—one of the things I love about you is your fighting spirit.' He kissed her lightly.

She sighed with satisfaction. 'I didn't really think you were going to be the kind of husband who laid down the law. That's why it came as such a shock, I suppose.'

'Well, I hope this doesn't come as too much of a shock but I'm about to lay down the law right now.'

She sat up and eyed him suspiciously.

He looked around at the lengthening shadows, and then at his watch. 'Dinner is not that far away. I don't see how we can get out of it, but there's nothing to prevent us from retiring early after it. So if you have any plans to be the perfect hostess this evening, Tattie—'

'Oh, I have plans, Alex,' she interrupted. 'To be the perfect something. But you'll just have to wait and see what that is.'

He raised an eyebrow. 'On the other hand, I may not be able to wait that long.' He looked at her narrowly. 'You're not about to become a law-laying-down kind of wife?'

'Wait and see,' she teased, then sobered suddenly.

'What?' he asked.

'I still can't believe it.' Tears suddenly glistened on her lashes.

He took her face in his hands and kissed them away. 'You will,' he promised. 'You will.'

Dinner was both a triumph and an ordeal.

They dressed up, Tattie in a long cream sheath with

a Chinese collar, Alex in dark trousers and a pale grey shirt.

Polly and Marie produced a splendid meal and all their guests were more than delighted, not only with the meal and the elegance but also with Tattie and Alex.

In fact, Tattie wondered if there was some visible aura around them. Then she knew there was, from the way Alex's dark eyes rested on her from time to time, and the way everything receded and all she was conscious of was him.

If she had any doubts, Polly dispelled them completely. 'Don't worry about staying around for the coffee,' she said to Tattie in a whispered aside, and impulsively threw her arms around her. 'I've never seen you looking so beautiful.'

Alex was waiting for her in the main bedroom. He had a silver tray, two glasses and a decanter of liqueur brandy, and he poured them a tot each and toasted her. Then he put the lights out and they stood side by side, holding hands, watching the moon rise over Beaufort before he turned to her.

'You had something you wanted to show me, Mrs Constantin?'

'Yes, this,' she said simply. She put her glass down. 'Although I may need some help.'

She turned around, and after a moment he began to release all the tiny buttons down the back of her dress. His fingers were cool on the skin of her back but he made no other attempt to touch her.

When the last button was released she stepped out of the dress and turned back to face him. 'And this,' she said softly. She took off her bra and stepped out of briefs then her shoes, and shivered slightly.

He put his arms around her. 'The perfect wife,' he

said huskily. 'Tattie, if only you knew how much I love you.'

And there was so much emotion in his eyes, something that was so hard held within him, at last full belief came to her.

'It's all right,' she said shakily, 'I know now.'

And he took her to bed.

It was around midnight when they stirred and Tattie sat up, disorientated, still on cloud nine over the events that had passed between them—the way Alex had made love to her so that not only their bodies but also their souls had been united.

'What is it?' she whispered.

He sat up and pushed his hair out of his eyes—and the sound came again. A scratch on the door... 'Oh,' he said, and at the same time she said.

'It's Oscar! But I thought Polly had trained him to sleep in the boot room?'

Alex grimaced and fingered his jaw. 'She had. I...liberated him last night.'

'You brought him in to sleep with you!'

'I did, I'm afraid,' Alex confessed.

'So much for your disapproval of my dog-training techniques,' Tattie said gravely. 'You realise he's probably *chewed* his way out of the boot room?'

'I was lonely and miserable.'

'I don't know why,' Tattie said severely, then fell back into his arms, laughing softly, 'but I love the sound of it!'

'You're a sadist, Tatiana.'

'No. It also makes me feel...really married to you!'

He took her chin in his hands and kissed her. 'Then it was worth it. What shall we do?'

'Let him in?' she suggested. 'Who knows what kind of havoc he could create out there.'

'But I have you now,' he pointed out, and ran his hands over her breasts.

'Alex, he's probably lonely and miserable out there. And you were the one who gave him to me.'

'For my sins,' he commented, and they both stopped as Oscar whined piteously. 'You know he's an awful fraud, don't you? He can turn his emotions on and off like a tap.'

'I won't be able to sleep if I know he's out there feeling sad.' Tattie looked sad herself. 'Besides which, he deserves to know all is well.'

'I see. You are going to be one of those law-laying-down kind of wives.'

'Only over this!'

'Promise?' He reached over and switched on the bed-side light.

'Well—'

'I thought so. So we'll need to think of a system of compensation.' His words were sober but his eyes were completely wicked.

Tattie took a breath. 'Oh, I get it. This is bribery and corruption.'

'It may be all that's left to me.'

'If you let Oscar in I'll…really rethink my stance on red-hot sex in the future.'

'Done,' he said promptly, and got out of bed to open the door.

Oscar raced into the room, leapt onto the bottom of the bed and snuggled down as if he'd come home.

And Tattie and Alex couldn't stop laughing, before they fell asleep in each other's arms.

The world's bestselling romance series.

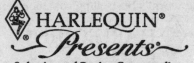

## HARLEQUIN®
### *Presents*
**Seduction and Passion Guaranteed!**

## Mama Mia!

ITALIAN HUSBANDS

They're tall, dark…and ready to marry!

Don't delay, pick up the next story in
this great new miniseries…pronto!

**On sale this month**
MARCO'S PRIDE by Jane Porter #2385

**Coming in April**
HIS INHERITED BRIDE by Jacqueline Baird #2385

**Don't miss**
**May 2004**
THE SICILIAN HUSBAND by Kate Walker #2393

**July 2004**
THE ITALIAN'S DEMAND by Sara Wood #2405

Pick up a Harlequin Presents® novel and you will
enter a world of spine-tingling passion and
provocative, tantalizing romance!

*Available wherever Harlequin books are sold.*

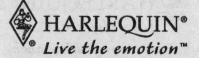

## HARLEQUIN®
### *Live the emotion*™

**Visit us at www.eHarlequin.com**

HPITHUSB

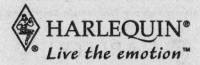

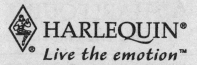

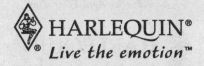

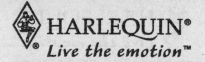

The world's bestselling romance series.

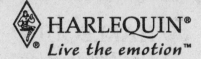